Stand-Up and Die

by

Pat Dennis

[signature: Pat Dennis]

Penury Press   Minneapolis

www.penurypress.com

First Edition

Library of Congress Card Number: 00-191811

Dennis, Pat

Stand-Up and Die

SUMMARY: Mystery novel featuring Mannie Grand, comedienne and amateur sleuth.

ISBN: 0-9676344-0-5

0 9 8 7 6 5 4 3 2 1

Printed in Canada

For

Martha Addison

You Are Marvelous

"The nice thing about being self-employed is that when your therapist tells you you're schizophrenic, you've doubled your staff." Mannie Grand, on-stage at The Laugh Inn.

1

"Bob Patterson died on-stage last night," my roommate and fellow comedienne LaVonne said as I stumbled half-awake into the kitchen. For some unknown reason my alarm had gone off at the ungodly early hour of 9:00 a.m.

LaVonne was filling a pig-shaped teakettle with water. She only likes pretend coffee — you know the kind — Swiss Chocolate Mocha Decaf Memories or Coffee Canals of Vienna Crappola. I began searching around for the hard stuff — espresso beans. Sometimes I didn't even bother to add water.

I was still dressed in my Minnesota winter sleep get-up — extra large red plaid flannel pajamas that were, due to late night pizza deliveries, quite snug. I also wore a green woolen plaid hat with the fur-lined flaps pulled down over my ears. I had forgotten to remove my large gold-plated hoop earrings from the night before. I must have looked like a transvestite lumberjack.

LaVonne was in her Eva Gabor of Green Acres lounging outfit — a long silk wanna-be rose-colored gown and matching robe, complete with white feathered lapels. LaVonne is petite, blond and beautiful. Despite those annoying flaws, we are best friends.

"Did you hear what I said about Bob?"

"Big deal," I mumbled sarcastically as I plugged in the 1950s percolator I had purchased at a garage sale for 10 cents. "Bob dies every time he's on-stage. He's gotta be the worst comic alive."

"Not anymore," she responded. "He's dead, as in dead. Really dead."

It took awhile for my mouth to work.

"You're not talking about bombing?" I asked, knowing by

then she wasn't.

"No," she answered. "I'm talking about murder."

I felt every cell of my body filling with dread. My clandestine activities for Bob the night before jumped into my mind. His death was my fault. I started shaking so bad I had to sit down.

That one personality trait of mine — the ability to take full responsibility for every action or reaction in the universe — is what makes me a good comedienne, a dependable friend, and a virtual gold mine for therapists. But this time my neurosis was based somewhat on fact. What I had done for Bob yesterday had to be part of the equation.

"He's dead dead?" I repeated LaVonne's words, trying to sound innocent. "Like in dead?"

"Like in killed," she answered. "The police said it looks like the food in the dressing room at The Comedy Box was poisoned."

I looked at her buttonnose face. For a change it wasn't perky. I lowered my head. I didn't want her to see my face. Guilt is a hard thing to hide. She had no idea of my illegal dealings with Bob.

"No one else was hurt?" I asked. LaVonne shook her head.

"Do they have any idea who did it?" I asked.

"Not that I know," she answered.

"I'll have to deal with this later," I told her, standing up. I wanted to get out of the room as soon as possible. All I wanted to do was to escape into sleep.

"I'm going to bed. I can't keep my eyes open anymore," I told her honestly. I edged my way toward my bedroom.

"Stop," she said firmly. I turned around.

"You can't go to bed," she continued as she pulled a box of Mongolian Mint Madness from the shelf.

"But I didn't get home last night until 4:30. I'm bushed."

"I set your alarm for a reason. They said they want to talk to us at ten this morning."

"Who are they?" I asked. I was so emotionally drained that I thought nothing in the world could keep me awake. I was wrong.

"They," she answered, "are the cops."

"The emcee this week at The Comedy Box is Bob Patterson, who once again proves that you don't have to be funny to be a comedian." City Pages review printed the morning before Bob Patterson's death.

2

"The Comedy Box — Proudly Voted Minnesota's 12th Entertainment Hot Spot" was brightly painted on a banner that hung over the entrance to the club's parking lot. The tiny lot was filled with squad cars and junkers. It looked as if every cop and comic in the Twin Cities had shown up to poke their noses into Bob's death. I, at least, had a legitimate reason to be there. I was afraid he was dead because of me.

Me, of all people, Amanda Mona Nora Grand, or Mannie, as I am called. Me, an overweight, divorced, childless, and marginally successful stand-up comedian. Me, a woman who drives below the speed limit and stops when a stoplight turns yellow, much less red. Me, a former Girl Scout (with two merit badges), was involved with murder.

LaVonne's voice shook me back to the moment. "Look who's here."

We watched as Tom Schneider, a somewhat animated octogenarian and ex-vaudevillian, hobbled down the sidewalk. Tom likes to joke he's only one good night with one bad woman away from death. Then we saw Jerry Callahan, another elder of the comedy world pull up in his rusty '78 Cadillac.

"All we need now is for Angela Lansbury to show up and it would be *Murder She Wrote* meets *The Sunshine Boys*," I joked lamely.

LaVonne didn't bother to smile at my pathetic attempt at humor. We both knew it was too soon for humor.

We skidded into a space. No one had bothered to scatter salt so I slid into the nearest car. I recognized it as my friend's Lenny's car. I wouldn't bother mentioning it to him. Between our two cars there were already over six dozen dents. Who could tell that another had been added?

LaVonne untangled the army blanket from around her size four body. With her blonde hair and near-perfect figure, she resembled a Barbie doll. I, who am as round as I am tall, was closer to a Cabbage Patch kid.

We're both into vintage clothes. Like most entertainers, LaVonne and I think the world is our stage and clothing our costumes. She reminded me of Veronica Lake in the '40s black rayon dress she was wearing. Earlier I had tried on my "WWII retro dress" and looked like Eleanor Roosevelt. I quickly changed into jeans, a white silk shirt, and black blazer. A somber but respectful look.

"When are you getting your heater fixed?" LaVonne snapped, pulling her red wool swirl coat tightly around her. She was using her glittered and glued-on Lee Press-On nails to scratch off the ice that had formed on the inside of the car window. She had been testy all morning but considering what she had gone through last night at the club, I thought she was doing well. She had also been one of the scheduled performers.

"When I get some money," I answered, which of course meant probably never. My car backfired and sputtered as I turned it off. I tapped the dashboard seven times for good luck — hoping that it would start again when we came out.

"Do you think there'll be donuts?" LaVonne asked. Earlier we hadn't felt like having anything to eat after discussing the fact that Bob had keeled over a minute or so after biting into a sandwich. Everyone assumed the food was poisoned.

"Dave never gives anything away. He's probably already hawking T-shirts of the crime scene."

"Or getting free publicity at least. There's the WXLZ van."

"Crap! Why didn't I bring my promo packet," I whined, noting how easily I jumped onto the "what's in it for me" bandwagon. If I've learned one thing from being in show business, it's that my ego is as big as anyone else's.

We got out of the car and walked across the parking lot. LaVonne's 3-inch lime-green high heels dug into the snow. The gray moon boots I was wearing flattened everything within a two-foot radius.

"I guess Bob's finally got his fifteen minutes of fame," I said solemnly as I opened the door to the club.

Bob Patterson had wanted fame as much as anyone I knew. At forty-nine, he was the hardest working, un-funniest man who ever hit a comedy stage. But one good thing you could always say about Bob; he was honest. He had to be. No one would steal material that bad.

I never asked Bob why he went into comedy. I barely understood why I did. My jokester origins surely had something to do with my coming from a long line of ruffians, scofflaws and swindlers. When I traced my roots for my seventh grade history project, I found most of my ancestors had been hung on one family tree or another. The few relatives I had left included a kind-hearted but gambling-addicted 77-year-old father and a shiftless, worthless, petty thief of a brother. Ironically, I was majoring in law enforcement before I dropped out of college when I was falsely accused of stealing from the activity fund. My family didn't bother to ask me if I did it. They just wanted to know how much I got.

With a family like mine, it seemed I had only two choices in life — either go insane or become a stand-up.

As I walked into the main room at The Comedy Box and saw the disheveled and neurotic ensemble that were my beloved peers, I felt completely at home. Every comedian I knew came from a screwed up background. We were always looking for love in all the wrong places and probably would until the day we died. Just like Bob.

A couple dozen comics were sitting at the tables, smoking, slurping down coffee and chomping on the day-old Swedish coffee cake that Dave had provided. I was wrong about Dave's generosity that morning but I knew I was right to be concerned about being asked to be there.

Two uniformed cops stood in the corner. There was no doubt in my mind that their eyes were focused on me and no one else.

Dave was scurrying around like the skinny little rat he was, setting up extra chairs. An unfiltered cigarette dangled from his mouth. He was wearing a three-piece black suit and gold tie.

Around his wrist he wore an 18-karat ID bracelet that was slightly larger than a bicycle chain. The bracelet clanked annoyingly against his Rolex watch. On his fingers were several large jeweled rings that resembled weaponry rather than embellishment. Topping him off was an unbelievably bad toupee. Because Dave owns a club that everyone wants to work, no one bothers to tell the emperor that not only is he naked, but he has really bad taste.

Originally, The Comedy Box was a sex joint called X World that provided topless dancing and bottomless sleaze, but as Dave pithily put it, "I ran sex into the ground, so I thought I'd give comedy a whirl."

That was in 1981, when comedy was at its peak. Dave Olson, in spite of being only five-foot-two, had become one of the biggest men in comedy in the upper Midwest.

LaVonne disappeared into the ladies room while I walked to the table where Bob's roommate, Lenny Milano, was slumped in a chair. Suddenly, the reason we were all there, the fact that Bob had been murdered, slammed into my chest. By the time I reached the chair next to Lenny, I could barely walk.

Lenny's orange-colored frizzy hair, hard to comb in the best of times, was sticking both up and sideways. His overwhelming sadness was apparent. He looked like a tall, unshaven, alcoholic, grieving leprechaun, which, unfortunately, he was.

Lenny's voice was not the deep baritone that one would expect from his operatic sounding name but that of a sweet Irish tenor. Twelve years ago, Lenny had changed his name from McMillan to Milano for what he called "box office draw." So far, it hadn't worked.

"I'm sorry, Lenny," I told him, realizing the limitations of even sincere condolences. "I know you and Bob were close friends. It's got to be tough."

"You have no idea," Lenny sighed loudly, managing to hold back a sob. "I still don't believe it."

"Neither do I," I told him. Part of me still expected Bob to walk through the door and yell "Surprise." The whole ugly business engulfed me again, along with my genetically based fear of incarceration. I started to tremble. I took a deep breath to calm myself down.

I desperately wanted to ask Lenny if he was aware of the favor Bob had asked me to do for him only a few hours before he died. But if Lenny didn't know about Bob's illegal activities, now was not the time to tell him. I was in enough hot water myself; I didn't want to drag Lenny down with me in the process.

"It's weird, isn't it?" another comic mumbled behind us. "First Tom Dilbert gets killed in a car crash and then Bob dies." Thirty-six hours earlier, the news of Dilbert's accident had been reported on the radio. Dilbert, a comic/magician from Seattle, was on a Midwest comedy club tour that included a week in Minneapolis at The Comedy Box and then a one-night performance in Duluth, one hundred fifty miles north. Dilbert was a good magician, but obviously not good enough to keep his car from leaving an ice-covered Highway 61 and driving straight into Lake Superior.

But I'm never surprised when a comic bites the big one on the road. As far as I was concerned, Dilbert had merely joined a long list of road dogs who had been killed while driving to or from a low paying gig. Comics are expected to show up for their performance, regardless of the weather. The old adage "the show must go on" is burned into our psyches.

"What have the cops told you?" I asked Lenny.

"They think the food was poisoned," Lenny answered, shaking his head in disbelief.

"Food poisoning?" I asked hopefully. Charley's Deli, the club's caterer, was hardly revered for its fine, or even good, cuisine. I had been praying that, if Bob had to die, it was from E-coli and not something more sinister, that could eventually connect itself to me.

"Cyanide," Lenny whispered.

Okay, so a lot of my prayers go unanswered.

"Testing! Testing!" Dave yelled into the microphone as he stood center-stage. He began to pound the side of the mike with his hand.

"What a jerk," I said, watching Dave bang relentlessly on the sensitive electronic equipment. Even if the equipment did come from Radio Shack, it deserved a little respect. "How many times do you think he's handled that mike? Thousands? And he still doesn't know where the on-button is?"

LaVonne returned and sat down across from Lenny and me. She leaned over and kissed him gently. The pheasant feather from the netted, purple pill-box hat she was wearing brushed against his hair.

"I'm so sorry about Bob," she said, as she squeezed Lenny's hand and added sincerely, "He was a wonderful guy."

She opened her purse and pulled out her last Virginia Slim cigarette. Then she put the empty package back into her purse. She saved the packaging so she could order the tobacco company's premiums. Every January she ordered a date book with the words "You've come a long way, baby!" imprinted on the front. I told her to make sure she saved enough coupons for the "You've come a long way baby" oxygen tank she'll eventually need.

"I'm surprised I didn't see this in the cards," LaVonne told Lenny, going into the flake mode she often uses to protect herself from reality. "I did a reading for Bob only two weeks ago."

LaVonne fancies herself a psychic and uses Tarot cards to predict the future with both amazing inaccuracy and total wackiness. At my last reading, she claimed that I have prison karma, due to a wicked but jail-free life I led during the 1700s and unless I was very careful, I would be locked away in this one.

I would have laughed it off, but I had a feeling that for once she was right. From birth (at least in this life) I have been the one who got the blame if something went wrong. In fact, if I hadn't been wrongfully accused of embezzling at my alma mater, I probably would have gotten my law enforcement degree and not be in my current mess. Or at least I'd be on the right side of it.

"Testing. Testing. Is it on? Is it working?" Dave asked, oblivious to all the nodding heads. "I'd like to thank all of you for coming. As you know, Bob Patterson died last night on this very stage."

I felt a stab of pain at Dave's crudeness. I looked around and saw that most of the comics were also in pain — not only at

Bob's death but because they were literally biting their lips to keep from making a wisecrack. Each and every one of them would have loved to make a remark about Bob's dying every night on that stage, but for once they were restraining themselves.

"In case you haven't already heard, the police are assuming, until the autopsy report comes back, that Bob was killed by poison hidden in Charley's Submarine Special."

Oh, the jokes! The one-liners! The witty quips that would have been uttered under different circumstances. Lips were being bitten so hard that many of the comics had tears in their eyes. I have never been so proud of them.

"As you know, I always provide my performers with a generous buffet...." Dave continued.

This was a bit too much for even the most noble of us. Coughs, gasps, and mumbled utterances of "Jesus Christ" and "I don't believe this" filled the room. Dave's backstage buffets were notorious.

The year before, Dave was forced into a financial stranglehold by a comedians' strike because he hadn't raised salaries since 1984. For two weeks, angry quipsters protested in front of his club until he agreed to make a change.

Claiming he was near bankruptcy, Dave announced that he could only give us another ten bucks a night for each performer but he would include a free meal.

The ten dollars quickly became five. The free meal, which ranged from two day-old bagels with dried crusty cream cheese to greasy take-out, was barely edible. What should have fed two people was stretched to feed three or four. Dave's favorite coupon deal was from Charley's, infamous for its $2.39 foot-long special.

It didn't even cost three dollars to kill Bob.

"Since the buffet was available only to me and last night's performers — Bob, LaVonne Hastings, and Grant Cuddler, we're not exactly sure who the killer was after," Dave continued.

Out of the four of them, my money was on Dave.

"WXLZ is planning a tribute to Bob on their six o'clock broadcast. LaVonne, why don't you go into the bar area where they can tape you? Also, Detective Brott would like to talk to some of the comics in my office. Let's see...."

My heart sank as I looked around at the others. Was it possible that any one of them knew the mess I was in and what I had done for Bob a few hours before he died?

Dave paused and dramatically looked over the waiting crowd. I slid deeper into my chair, trying to make myself as inconspicuous as possible.

"Mannie" he said, as my last bit of my luck ran out, "You first."

"I was fired from the only corporate job I ever held. My boss said I had an attitude problem because I wore a suit on casual days." Mannie Grand live at CoCoNuts' Comedy Club.

3

Dave's office was slightly bigger than my bathroom, yet three policemen were crammed into it with me. I noticed my hands were shaking, so I crossed my arms and placed each one under an armpit. It was then I noticed my perspiration had soaked through my clothes.

It was already too late for the old show biz maxim, "Never let them see you sweat."

One of the policemen stood blocking the door. I'm claustrophobic and immediately started looking at the window for a way out of the room. I always need to know every exit. I knew I looked like I wanted to bolt, which, of course, I did, but the room was too small and the cops too close.

In the center of the room, Dave's desk rested on a platform that was built a foot higher than the rest of the floor. The six-foot-wide metal desk, painted to simulate mahogany, held a quill pen in a fake crystal inkwell. It was Dave's attempt to add class that both the decor and Dave were missing. The desk itself was positioned like a fortress ready for war.

Directly behind it was Dave's chair. On it usually sat a three-inch high tapestry seat cushion with Dave on top of that. The chair was the size of a small throne. It was from that vantage point that Dave controlled his little kingdom. But for once, His Royal Pain had allowed a police investigator to sit where no one else had ever sat. Until the killer was found, it was obvious that the new King on the block was Detective Brott.

If it had been a movie about Bob's death, and not reality, and I wanted it to be a silly romance rather than a deadly mystery, I would cast Detective Brott in the role he was playing.

He was tall and muscular with light brown hair streaked with silver. His dark green eyes were what I would call emerald green, if I were inclined to be the romantic type. Like Sean Connery or Dick Clark, he was one of the blessed few who would never appear to age. I assumed he was in his mid-forties, but I could almost swear that he was twenty-something. He was drop-dead gorgeous.

But it was more than his looks that intrigued me. I sensed an immediate connection when our eyes met, as if I had known him before and would know him from then on. But then I reminded myself that I felt the same way in high school when I saw Davy Jones of The Monkees on TV for the first time. And Davy and I have yet to meet.

I decided I was suffering from a case of chocolate deficiency. I've noticed I care less about men after eating a Baby Ruth. I leaned back against the wall, amazed that even with all of these major emotions — grief, despair, and terror — when I looked at Brott, I could still fit in lust. I wondered briefly if it was close to my "time of the month" and the few eggs I had left were spinning out of control.

My head rested against a twenty-year-old black and white photograph of Jay Leno. There were hundreds of headshots taped across the walls. Thousands more were piled on the floor along with innumerable audition tapes. At last count, the IRS said there were five thousand citizens who claimed to be professional comedians. Apparently all of them had, at one time or another, contacted The Comedy Box.

I felt myself becoming disoriented and wondered if I was going to faint until I realized that my sense of balance had been thrown off by the rickety pine chair I was sitting on. Except for his own chair and desk, Dave Olson had shortened the legs of everything in his office.

"So, you're a comic?" Brott asked in a tone suggesting that if I answered yes, I would be lying.

"Sure," I answered, a bit startled by being brought back to reality by both his question and skepticism. I was used to justifying my career. I scanned the room for my headshot. Most people don't understand that you can earn a living as an entertainer and still not be famous.

Finally, I saw my photo taped on the far wall, half hidden

behind a Hooters' wall calendar. The half that was visible was almost covered with Post-it notes.

"There I am," I said, pointing to the barely visible 8x10 glossy, relieved that at least the first of my answers to Brott could be proven.

Brott reached over and took my photo off the wall. He removed the Post-its and stared at it. He looked at me, then turned back to the photo in apparent disbelief.

"This is a little old, isn't it?" he asked, and then had the grace to be embarrassed that he had been so rude.

"The photo's a few years old," I said, not admitting that I also weighed forty pounds less when it was taken. I never acknowledge my weight or age. The fact that I am forty-one, female and fat in a male-dominated business is hardly a plus.

Brott turned over the photograph and began to read the lengthy bio printed on the back. "You were on The Phil Donahue Show?" he asked. "When was that?"

"1982," I answered, still embarrassed, after almost two decades, by that day.

"Were you an audience member?"

"I was a guest comic," I answered. "They held auditions for new talent and I won a three-minute time slot."

"That was a pretty big deal, wasn't it? If you don't mind my asking, why aren't you a star?"

"I have no idea," I told him. But, of course, I did. My first and only major television appearance was a disaster. Instead of being focused on my act, my mind was on problems at home. That morning, my brother, Chet, had been arrested on a felony charge of drug dealing. My mom had died only three weeks earlier. And Dad had informed me by phone, five minutes before I was to perform, that he had spent his entire paycheck on pull-tabs and didn't have money for his mortgage payment.

My performance was totally unprofessional. When I look back at it, I think I was still numb from mom's death, much less the other problems that were surfacing. I had stumbled through every punch line.

And because of my bumbling, I blew my one chance to save what was left of my family. If it had gone well, I could have hired the best lawyers for Chet, put Dad in treatment for his gambling problem, and bought Mom a decent tombstone. Instead, my debut became, in a way, my finale.

One day later, I found myself in Las Vegas, standing at the craps table, giving birth to my own self-destructive, addictive behavior. The true Grand in me had started to emerge. I was carrying on the family tradition that the only thing to do after messing up, was to mess up even more.

"Did you know the deceased well?" Brott asked. I looked up at him, remembering where I was and why I was there.

"You mean Bob?" I asked, annoyed that Bob was being referred to as the deceased. "Sure, I knew him. I'd sit with him on Open Mike Night at the club. We went on a few road gigs together," I said, closing my eyes and resisting the image of Bob lying on the stage, choking out his last breath.

"Where?"

"Twice to North Dakota and once to Chicago."

"When was the last time?"

"Two years ago," I answered, feeling guilty, wondering if the list of emotions I was feeling would ever stop growing. Bob had begged me for jobs but I had stopped using him two years ago. As a headliner I was usually awarded the courtesy of choosing who I would work with and Bob just wasn't funny enough. I was tired of having to work extra hard to remind an audience they were there to laugh, after Bob had convinced them otherwise.

But like most comics, it never once crossed Bob's mind that he wasn't as funny as he thought he was. Besides, he had proof that he was funny. Wasn't there that one evening when no matter what he said or did, the crowd roared?

"Was Bob into drugs?" Brott asked, bringing me back from my thoughts.

"Not that I was aware of," I said, hoping that by "drugs" Brott meant the hard stuff. "I'm sure he did an occasional joint or two but I think he was more into food than anything else."

Bob, like myself, dealt with being physically big in a small world. It was one of the reasons we seldom worked together. Nothing scared a club owner like too many fat jokes.

"What about sex?"

"I don't know anything about Bob's sex life," I answered, wondering if Brott would ask the male comics the same question. Why was everything usually connected to sex?

"Did he ever come on to you?" Brott asked.

"No," I answered honestly. Bob was one of the few men I knew who seemed truly asexual.

"Were you attracted to him?"

I was becoming embarrassed at Brott's line of questioning. It was one thing to stand on-stage and make jokes about sex but quite another to talk about it in private.

"He wasn't my type," I answered truthfully. I've noticed that we corpulents are as prone as anyone to the seduction of stereotypical slimness as beauty. I'm more likely to swoon over Mel Gibson than John Goodman — yet I bet Goodman is better in bed. If Gibson had a mirror on the ceiling, it would probably only be to check out his hair.

"Did any of the comics ever talk to you about Bob?"

"Not any more than they talked about everyone else," I said. Comics talk about comics all the time. Bob's name always seemed to come up when the bantering started. There were always complaints about how Bob's act was boring and not funny. There were unfounded innuendoes and snide comments about him and his relationship with his roommate, Lenny. But I didn't tell Brott any of this. To me, the talk was just comic gossip and not worthy of repeating, even to the cops.

"Did anyone hate him?"

In the comedy world, if you want to be liked by your peers, it's best not to be too funny. "Everyone liked Bob," I said honestly.

"Were you at The Comedy Box last night?" Brott asked, pulling a cigarette out of his pocket, placing it in his mouth, but not lighting it.

"No," I answered, wondering why he didn't bother to light it. Maybe he was trying to quit. Maybe he thought a cigarette made him look tough. Maybe he thought a cigarette made him look sexy. Maybe it did.

"Why weren't you at the show? Wasn't your roommate, LaVonne, performing?" he asked as he glanced at his notes that

19

obviously already contained a great deal of personal information about me.

"I've seen LaVonne's act a hundred times. Besides, going to a comedy club is like going to work and I never go to work on my day off. Do you?"

For the first time, Brott almost smiled. "I never take a day off when I'm on a case," he said. He looked at me sternly, his eyes once again unfriendly. He was changing emotions so quickly and putting me through the ringer so expertly, in such a short time, that I wondered why we had never met before. He was exactly the kind of man I was used to dating: one second he was charming, the next cold and controlling.

"Where were you last night?" he asked.

My gut tightened. "I was home reading," I answered, squirming in my seat and wondering if he had enough experience to know I wasn't telling the truth. Then, with the skeptical look he gave me, I knew he did.

"Mannie, do you know what a man usually says when he's dying?" Brott asked, twirling a number ten pencil around in his hand.

"What man?" I asked, glancing toward the window. Would my thighs fit through it if I had to make an escape?

"Any dying man. I've seen enough to know. It's kind of ironic; the last words of tough guys, rapists, and serial killers is usually 'Momma.' "

"So?" I answered sharply, not wanting to hear that Bob called out for his mom.

"However, once in a while we good guys get lucky," Brott continued, increasing my discomfort. "Once in a great while, the dying man whispers his killer's name."

I've written enough bad jokes to see a set-up coming a mile away. I looked back at the door, The cop was still standing in front of it. There was no way out.

"Would you like to know Bob's last word?" he asked.

My throat suddenly went dry. I couldn't speak. I barely nodded my head. Brott broke the pencil in two that he had been twirling. He looked at me and repeated Bob's last word.

"Mannie."

"For a comedian, I have a great retirement plan. Well, it's The Publishers Clearinghouse Sweepstakes. Hey, don't laugh! I'm in The Final Stage." Mannie Grand, live at The Comedy Box.

4

Brott had watched closely for my response as he dropped Bob's last word. For the first time, my unwanted gambling gene became a blessing. I knew he could tell nothing from my poker face. He waited several minutes in silence before he nodded, indicating to me that I was free to leave.

I walked out of Dave's office with my head held high and my shoulders tossed back defiantly. My stomach, sucked in for appearance sake, was, however, churning like a Cuisinart. I sat back down at Lenny's table and grabbed the half empty coffee cup I had left, gulped it down too fast, and immediately started coughing.

The Kid walked over and started patting me on the back. "You okay?" he asked as he sat down.

Everyone calls him either Kid or The Kid. Most of us have forgotten his real name, but it doesn't matter. The Kid is how he'll always be known. At eighteen years of age, he is funnier and brighter than the rest of us will ever be. Three L.A. talent scouts have already flown to Minneapolis to catch his act. LaVonne runs a pool on when he'll make his first national TV appearance. She has three bucks riding that he'll be on Leno by fall.

None of us were surprised at his early success. We all love him. The only catch is that we all hate him too. We're pissed that he'll never have to pay his dues. The rest of us will be stuck doing crappy one-nighters in North Dakota for the rest of our lives. We'll pay his dues for him.

"I'm okay," I said, grabbing a glass of water.

The Kid pulled out a box of Tic Tacs and popped a couple of

21

mint greens.

"Have a few," he said, handing the box to me.

"Thanks, Kid," I answered.

"Too bad about Bob gettin' killed," The Kid said to Lenny, his social skills not yet on the same maturity level as his comedy.

"Yeah," Lenny answered. I could tell Lenny's patience was wearing thin. Minute by minute he was looking more tired and alone.

The Kid tossed another Tic Tac high in the air and caught it open-mouthed. "How come Cuddler's not here?"

I looked around and realized for the first time that last night's headliner hadn't shown up.

"I have no idea," I answered. "Lenny, do you know?"

"Haven't a clue," Lenny said. I noticed small beads of sweat had formed on his forehead. Dave had turned up the heat, for a change, but it wasn't that hot in the club.

"I was hoping to talk with Cuddler," The Kid whined. "I'm going to be on the West Coast in the spring. I thought he could give me a few tips."

I gave The Kid a look. It worked. I wanted him to remember why we were there in the first place. A peer and friend had been killed. We weren't there to push our careers.

I saw LaVonne coming across the room. She stopped at a few tables along the way. She was smiling but as she neared our table she became quieter, out of respect for Lenny. We were all treating Lenny like he was Bob's family. As far as we knew, he was the only family Bob had. It wasn't unusual for a comedian to have no one except the comedy community.

I looked around the room filled with neer-do-wells and wanna-bes, grown-up class clowns who hadn't yet realized there are more important things in life to do than making fools of ourselves.

I longed for the '80s when the best and the brightest went out for stand-up. By the mid-'90s, most working comedians were too embarrassed to say what they did for a living, stand-ups had become so disrespected. One of the nastier theatre critics in town referred to us as "the bottom-feeders of the art world."

I looked up and saw that LaVonne was through with her

media interview and was walking toward us. Her eyes were filled with rage.

"I'm glad that's over with," LaVonne said as she sat down. She reached over and grabbed the bronze-colored coffee thermos and poured herself a cup.

"How bad was it?" I asked, wondering if she was upset because she had to share her grief on camera or if the interviewer was a jerk. As usual, it was the interviewer.

"Betty the Bimbo asked her standard idiot questions," LaVonne complained.

"Like what?"

"What makes a comedian funny? Is it inner pain from your inner child?" LaVonne said, doing an accurate imitation of the inane reporter.

We all groaned. Each of us had been asked a similar question a thousand times.

"What else?"

"She also asked if it was true that comedians were laughing on the outside but crying on the inside."

"Did you tell her to piss off?" The Kid asked.

"I should have. Her last question was the worst," LaVonne said, her mood changing to sadness.

"What was it?" I asked.

"She wanted to know if Bob was as unfunny as she had heard?"

"Did you tell the truth?" The Kid asked, his social skills once more failing him. He didn't even notice the hurt look on Lenny's face.

"I told her to go to hell," LaVonne laughed. "I think I'll be edited out. She said I have an attitude problem."

"No, you don't. You just hate her fake sincerity," I told her.

Lenny hit his fist on the table. "Betty Ivan didn't give a flying fig about Bob when he was alive. He could have used the publicity then, not now."

"But he wasn't a story when he was alive," mumbled Milos The Magnificent, as he pulled up a chair and sat down. Milos was the only bad magician I knew who also had the unique distinction of being an even worse comic.

Our table was becoming more crowded. Susan Vass and Heidi Honkamp sat down. Susan was already a nationally known name. Heidi was the prettiest comedian in town. As always, she was bright-eyed, funny and eager. If the fates allowed it, she, too, would become a star.

The circle around our table grew and grew and within a few minutes was one big group discussion. For a change, the conversation wasn't about what each of us was doing. Instead, it was loving tales about Bob.

Each one of us started telling Bob stories. We laughed at most, wiped away tears at a few, and didn't even notice that our mourning process had begun.

"Last month I borrowed twenty bucks from Bob. I found out later he had sold plasma that morning for a few dollars himself," The Kid said with reverence. "He never mentioned it to me."

"He'd do anything for a friend," Lenny continued, "or anyone else in need. One Christmas he found a wallet with three hundred dollars in it."

"And he returned it?" I asked.

"Of course. He said he could tell from the address on the ID inside the wallet that the owner was probably poor. He said if the guy was a rich bastard from Edina he would have kept it,"

"Do you remember the time Bob hosted Open Mike Night with his zipper open?" I asked.

Once again the laughter started. Tears began to roll down our faces as we remembered Bob standing on-stage, his zipper down, his face beaming.

"He had no idea he was flapping in the wind," I continued. "No one told him what was up...."

"Or down," LaVonne corrected.

"Every time he walked on-stage the crowd went nuts," I reminded everyone.

"Bob always bragged about that evening when he was a comedy god," Lenny told us.

We all laughed one more time and then collectively sighed, as if remembering why we were there and the fact that, although we had many, there would be no more Bob stories to tell.

At least I thought there wouldn't be.

"My new diet requires that I walk off any excess calories the same day I eat them. So basically I have to walk to Cleveland by midnight." Mannie Grand, on-stage at Sir Laughs-A-Lot, Milwaukee.

5

Nine hours after the interrogation by Brott I was in my apartment dropping pasta into a large stockpot filled with bubbling water. Cooking could easily become another compulsion for me, just like eating or gambling.

I have been "clean" as we like to say in G.A. (Gamblers Anonymous) for 3 years, 7 months, and 12 days. And yes, I am counting.

Being "clean" means I do not gamble. I do not go to the track. I do not buy lottery tickets. I do not enter the Publishers Clearinghouse Sweepstakes. I don't gamble. Period. I am in recovery. And with it comes a bit of serenity. The only problem is that I have also discovered that I miss gambling. Big time.

I miss the slot machines, the bright lights, the tinkling sounds of coins hitting the metal hopper. I miss knowing that any minute, even though I've already lost hundreds, I could score big. I miss watching my filly round the track to the finish line — usually in last place. I miss the thrill of the moment.

Part of me wondered if that was why I was willing to place the biggest bet of my life — that I could find Bob's killer on my own. Whatever the reason, the investigation had started the minute I invited Lenny to dinner.

As soon as we arrived at the apartment, LaVonne had changed into a more comfortable outfit. She was wearing her "Tammy Goes Butch" ensemble — an extra large man's white shirt, jeans, and thick wool socks worn with Birkenstock sandals. Her pig-tailed hair was tied with purple ribbons. She was standing near me as she chopped Romaine lettuce and vine-ripened tomatoes into small pieces.

Lenny had arrived a few minutes earlier. He sat patiently at our kitchen table. The three of us were wiped out. We had been at The Comedy Box until late afternoon. I had also asked Milos The Magnificent to join us but he refused. He'd kept his distance since LaVonne had ended their relationship a few months earlier. I peeled another garlic bulb as Lenny unscrewed the bottle of wine he had brought. Like most comics, he was on a limited budget, yet he loved giving presents.

"You've kept the popcorn!" Lenny said, smiling as he noticed the two-gallon bucket of holiday popcorn that sat on the counter. He and Bob had given it to us just a few weeks ago for Christmas.

"Sure," I smiled at him.

LaVonne and I weren't interested in eating the pail's contents. Neither one of us found chemically-dyed red and green kernels appealing. But the bucket it came in was decorated with Mickey as Santa Claus and Minnie as the Mrs. Besides, I knew Lenny wouldn't want us to destroy the package it came in.

In his best John Wayne voice, Lenny drawled, "You know, Little Missy, if you want it to go up in value, don't be a taking off the shrink wrap."

Lenny is an avid collector of Disney memorabilia. Although he could use the cash, like most collectors he'd never think of selling any of his cherished pieces. Walking into his apartment is like stepping into Disneyland.

When he performs, Lenny always wears a tie printed with cartoon designs or a T-shirt with at least one animated character on it. Lenny's an impressionist and does "voices" in his act ranging from Goofy to Bill Clinton, which, as LaVonne points out in her act, is not that far a stretch.

I smelled smoke coming from the broiler and realized that the first round of garlic bread had just burned to a crisp. I threw it out and started another batch. LaVonne started to toss a salad. I was pleased that Lenny had brought red wine. It would go well with the spaghetti marinara.

I had purchased the pasta sauce with a manufacturer's coupon. Two jars cost me $1.98. The pound of pasta cost 84¢. The day-old French bread that I covered with sautéed garlic and olive oil was 49¢ at the bakery outlet. The dinner's total cost was $3.31, a bit more than Lenny paid for the gallon of wine.

"Do you want to go to the funeral with us?" I asked Lenny, as he poured himself a second glass of wine.

"I can't. I need to leave that morning for The Funny Bone in Indianapolis."

"God, that's a good gig," I sighed, envious of Lenny's working at such a well-known comedy spot. I'm always amazed that no matter what I was feeling — anger, betrayal, fear — professional jealousy could always find a way to the top of the pyramid of emotions.

"You got that right. Two solid weeks at an "A" Club. I have died and gone to heaven..."

Lenny halted as he realized the inappropriateness of his comment. "Oh, Jesus, what a crappy thing to say at a time like..."

"Forget about it, Lenny," LaVonne reassured him. "Mannie and I will be at the funeral. We'll tell you all about it."

"You know I'd be there if I could. Bob was my..." Lenny trailed off sadly. Lenny was originally from the south side of Chicago and added "you know" to almost every sentence. To fit in to Minnesota, all he had to do was put the "you" at the end of the sentence instead, and add a "betcha."

"We understand, Lenny," I said, knowing what it's like to lose someone you love, but also knowing what it's like to lose a well-paying gig. "I wonder how many comics will show up for the funeral?"

"Every one of them. There's a free lunch, remember?" LaVonne said, as she placed our mismatched dishes and tarnished silverware on the table. "Besides, Bob was very well liked."

"I'm still in shock that Dave's paying for the funeral," I said, using a pasta fork to lift the strands out of the boiling water. "I'm beginning to think that he might be human after all."

"I wouldn't go that far," LaVonne said. She's always more cautious about men than I am, but then she has to be. Most of them are after her.

"You want me to do anything to help?" Lenny asked.

"No, just sit there and talk to us," I told him, wanting to get to the real reason I had invited him. I hadn't planned the evening to be a social event.

"I thought this might be a good time to compare notes on what happened last night," I said to both him and LaVonne.

"Mannie fancies herself an amateur sleuth," LaVonne giggled, giving away any chance I had for subterfuge.

"I could see you doing that," Lenny said, as he poured more wine for himself.

"She majored in law enforcement until she was accused of embezzling college funds," LaVonne announced lightheartedly, as if my once being charged with a felony was an everyday occurrence.

"I could see you as an embezzler," Lenny said with half a smile. I couldn't tell if he was teasing or not.

"I was acquitted," I stated firmly, giving LaVonne my "that's the last time I ever tell you any secrets" look. Even though I was proven totally innocent of any wrongdoing, it still wasn't a story that I wanted tossed about. I had no interest in being known as the Bad Girl of Comedy.

"Just tell me about the events of last night. You start, LaVonne."

I had heard her story on the drive to The Box but I wanted to hear it again and again. The one thing my criminology professor had stressed was that everyone usually forgets something and you need to ask the same questions over and over.

LaVonne rolled her eyes and then began in her silliest German accent, "Okay, I'll play your little game, Mein Sherlock. As you know, I vas vorking last night as the middle act between Bob and Grant Cuddler. I vas excited to be there. I've alvays vanted to meet Herr Cuddler. His routines are classic, mein little sauerkrauts,"

Thankfully, she continued on in her real voice. "I had heard he was twenty-two years old when he made his first appearance on The Tonight Show. I wanted to find out how he'd lost everything and ended up playing "B" rooms like The Box.

"Of course there are dozens of rumors as to why that happened. Some people say it was because of drugs. Another tale going around is that he was blacklisted because he seduced the daughter of a major Hollywood player."

"I heard it was the producer's wife," I interjected.

"I heard it was the producer's mother," Lenny laughed.

"Then there's the rumor about his nervous breakdown in Vegas," LaVonne added. "He was performing at the Comedy Stop at the Tropicana when he started yelling on-stage that he was nothing but a loser and a fraud. The audience kept waiting for the punch line. It took security ten minutes to figure out it wasn't a part of his act and drag him offstage."

"That's not gossip," Lenny told us as he topped off his tumbler again. "It's a fact. I've known Grant for years."

"I didn't know that," I said as I placed a large bowl of pasta on the table, wondering why Lenny hadn't mentioned this fact before. Comedians name-drop as often as they breathe. "How long?"

"His entire career. I was there the first time he went on-stage."

Lenny, like a lot of comics, had moved to the Twin Cities during the comedy boom. In the early '80s, cities like Chicago or New York had too many comics and not enough clubs. In the Twin Cities, a comic could get enough stage time to develop an act. Most of the comics planned to hone their material as quickly as possible and head to L.A. A few of them, like Lenny, never left. There was nothing special about Lenny's act. He'd never go farther than Omaha.

"How good was he the first time up?" I asked.

"He killed," Lenny responded, a fair amount of anger coming through his tone of voice. "It made me mad then and it makes me mad now. I've worked my tail off for years and I'm still not as good as Grant was his first time up. But I guess there's always a few that are funny from the first moment, like Bill Cosby..."

"Or Joan Rivers," I added, taking the opportunity to remind any him females are funny. Most male comics don't think women are funny. But maybe that's because a lot of female comics spend most of their time on-stage making fun of a man's most prized possession — and I'm not talking a Corvette — though I am talking small and way-too-fast.

"Grant was brilliant from day one," Lenny continued. "An agent signed him up the second he walked off the stage."

"When did the rumors about him being an ego-maniac start?" I asked, knowing that a lot of comics try to shoot their competition out of the water any way they can. Gossip can be more powerful than a semi-automatic.

"Almost immediately. It's not all gossip. Some of the tales are true. Even as a young punk, Grant had a dark side."

"Did you tell Bob what he was like?"

"Warned him was more like it. Bob was timid. I figured Grant would run over him and use him any way he could from bumming money to getting women for him. But Bob couldn't have cared less. He was glad to be working, even though he was only getting a hundred bucks."

"For each show?"

"For the whole week. Dave even fed him the old bullshit about 'You never know who might be in the audience.'"

"Obviously not," I noted, shivering as I wondered if the killer stayed to watch Bob die. "LaVonne, what time did you arrive at the club?"

"I was there by 7:30. There were only a few people in the house when I arrived. The crowd was so small that I wondered if there would even be an eight o'clock show."

"Was Bob already there?" I asked.

"Yep, he and Lenny were backstage," she said, looking at Lenny.

"I gave Bob a lift to the club," Lenny added. "You know how he is about driving."

I decided not to correct Lenny's use of tense in talking about Bob. I knew it would take a while for all of us to think of Bob in the past tense.

"Was Bob acting strange?" I asked.

Lenny looked at me and started laughing and then LaVonne and I joined in. Finally we stopped and Lenny sighed, "You know Mannie, that was priceless. Even Bob would be cracking up. Do you think he could have acted any way except strange?

"He was completely anal, yet, at the same time, a total slob, Every shirt he owned was covered with food stains but his shoes were always spit-shined. He never remembered to wash his hair but he had a professional manicure every week at the beauty school. A manicure, can you believe that? And he was only earning fifteen grand a year."

"It's true, Bob was a bit of an odd duck, but then what comic isn't?" I asked, taking a second helping of pasta, still feeling the need for lots of comfort. "Stand-up is a magnet for anyone with a problem. The more problems they have, the faster they fly to comedy. Have you ever known a truly sane comic?"

"Before or after recovery?" LaVonne asked.

It's a subject that LaVonne and I talk about all the time — how nuts most comics are. They are usually drug or alcohol addicted, often gambling fools, most likely descendants of dysfunctional families — pathetic, lonely, bitter, cynical, angry and disillusioned. Of course, it's always the other comics, not us, that are so screwed up. Or so we tell each other.

"Were the sub sandwiches there when you arrived, LaVonne?" I asked. I quivered a little when I again realized that she could have been the one killed.

"No, they weren't. There was only a pot of coffee and some chips."

"Were you there when Charley dropped off the subs?" I asked Lenny.

"I was out in front," Lenny answered.

"Did anyone else come backstage?" I asked LaVonne.

"Just Dave, that I know of," she said, remembering. "Charley brought the package of sandwiches, laid them out on the table and left. He only said a brief hello."

"That's odd for Charley," I told LaVonne. "He usually talks up a storm."

"I heard Dave chew Charley out for being late," Lenny said. "Charley was probably embarrassed."

"Or pissed off," LaVonne added.

"Did you leave the dressing room at all?"

"Come to think of it, I did," LaVonne said, remembering a part she had left out of her previous story. But then, maybe I hadn't remembered to ask the right question. "I went to the john."

31

"If Lenny was out front and you, LaVonne, were in the can, there's a block of time where we have no idea if anyone was backstage."

"We're talking a few minutes at the most," LaVonne said.

"It would have only taken a few minutes to lace the sandwich," I reminded her.

"Don't forget, Bob was backstage," Lenny added.

"How do we know that for sure? We can't ask him," I reminded Lenny, as if I needed to. "Even if Bob was there, maybe someone could have done it without his noticing."

"That would take balls," LaVonne said bitterly.

"This murderer had balls the size of New York. Thank God you didn't grab part of the sandwich." It was lucky she was a vegetarian.

"You know I never eat before the show."

"When did Grant get there?" I asked LaVonne.

"Just a few minutes before the show started," LaVonne answered.

I tried to get the events straight in my head. Dave was already at the club when Bob and Lenny arrived. LaVonne showed up right before Charley arrived with the sandwiches. Grant was the last to arrive.

"In fact, he was really grumpy," LaVonne continued. "When Bob asked Grant how he wanted to be introduced, Grant rattled off a pretty stock intro — you know — 'has worked clubs and colleges around the country.'"

"Didn't he want his Tonight Show credits announced?" Lenny asked, knowing that if a comic sits in the bleachers at a televised Yankees game, he'll add, "As seen on NBC's Wide World of Sports" to his list of credentials.

"No, in fact, when Bob asked about *The Tonight Show* credit, Grant nearly bit his head off," LaVonne told us.

"Maybe he's embarrassed by it," I offered, thinking about my own national television fiasco.

"Whatever the reason, I could have killed Grant when he snapped at Bob," LaVonne informed us. "Bob looked terrified. In fact, I think that's why he reached over and grabbed a section of the sandwich right before he went on-stage. He needed some comforting."

"Did Grant say anything to you when Bob went on?"

"No. He just kept staring at my boobs. It was only a few minutes until I heard Lenny yelling Bob's name."

"I was sitting at the front table," Lenny told us. "You know, at first I thought he was kidding around, but when he keeled over, I knew it was no joke."

"By the time Grant and I ran on-stage, I knew Bob was dying," LaVonne added, shuddering at her memory. "At first I thought it was a heart attack. But then, somehow, I just knew that it was the sandwich. I thought it was probably the E-coli thing you hear about. It was then that I did something really stupid. I didn't want anyone else to die, so I ran back to the dressing room and threw the sandwich in the garbage."

"But someone did touch it." I said.

"Someone certainly did. By the time the police arrived, the sandwich was missing," she sighed.

"And that someone," I announced, "was undoubtedly the same sonofabitch who drenched it in cyanide."

"Weird, isn't it?" Lenny asked in a voice that was almost emotionless.

"What?" I asked as I watched him suck down the last strand of spaghetti.

"Bob said that the only way he'd ever be famous would be to get killed in a freak accident."

"When did he say that?" I asked.

"You know, come to think of it, just a few hours before he died."

"They obviously do not have a lot of entertainment in North Dakota. Last time I was there I was introduced as a stand-up Canadian." Mannie Grand, ABC Millwork Employee Party.

⑥

Ramen noodles are the macaroni and cheese of today. When the Mac & Cheese became too white bread for the era of Generation X, Ramen noodles, hinting of the Orient, offered an illusion of diversity. I buy Ramen noodles because they are cheap. Twenty-two cents a package even before they go on sale. On sale, I can usually get seven packages for a buck. That's only 14 cents for 319 calories, 19 grams of fat, and a death-wish amount of sodium.

LaVonne and I pool our food money. Some weeks I'm on the road, some weeks she is, so we figure it all works out in the end.

We can usually afford a couple pounds of pasta, two jars of sauce, peanut butter, grape jelly, bread, eggs, popcorn, cheese, granola, a couple pounds of meat for me, tofu and nuts for LaVonne, and Ben & Jerry's for both of us. If we ever become rich, our money will be spent on cardiac specialists.

I do all the shopping. LaVonne, who once worked as a supermarket cashier, hates to walk into a grocery store. Besides, she is always watching her weight. I, who have vowed to never again diet, love the SuperValu.

It was a little after 8:00 a.m. when I arrived at the market. The store was filled with both the elderly and students. The SuperValu ran a daily bus from the Loring Senior Center. It was also a few blocks from Augsburg College.

My compulsive, almost daily, visits fulfill a tribal need of mine. I view it as a communal gathering of foods and fuel, conveniently wrapped in plastic and paper.

Also, as soon as I put my hands on the shopping cart, I feel like an adult. It was one of the few joys of my childhood — the feeling of being an adult when my mom thought I was big enough to push the cart for the first time — that has stayed with me.

I methodically started going through each department, beginning with produce. I like touching, feeling, squeezing and knocking on each fruit and vegetable. I have always assumed that if I ever get a permanent boyfriend, my obsession with zucchini and such will end.

I walked down each aisle slowly. I wanted to make my time at the SuperValu count. I was still shaken by both Brott's interrogation the day before and by the dinner LaVonne and I had shared with Lenny.

Throughout the meal there was something, beyond Bob's death, that seemed to be bothering Lenny. Small beads of sweat would form on his upper lip. He would begin to stutter and then stop and stare off into space. The few times our telephone rang he jumped.

He stayed until midnight, giving us no insight into the internal trauma he was trying unsuccessfully to hide. LaVonne and I were up talking about his actions until I finally crashed at 2:00 a.m. I tossed and tumbled most of the night, unable to sleep because of the bloody mess I was in.

At 7:00 a.m., a nightmare woke me to harsh reality. In the dream, LaVonne was sitting at the counter at Charley's Deli. She was munching on a birthday cake that was iced in blood. I was standing outside the window, pounding on the glass, begging her to stop. But no one heard me except Bob, who was floating over my head, dressed in a high-hat and tails. He kept repeating, "It's too late, Mannie. It's too late for any of us."

Knowing I couldn't go back to sleep, I headed out to the sanctity of the SuperValu to return my mind to a logical track. I needed to think about solutions rather than problems.

The SuperValu was a perfect place to do so. I could easily spend two hours shopping for just thirty buck's worth of food. I looked at each display, read almost every package in the store and fantasized about exotic meals I could make, if I were so inclined, and had more than $30.

I rarely cook anything gourmet. Efficiency in cooking has

always been the issue with me. And it's always quantity, not quality. I would still be grilling a hot dog by laying it directly on the electric burners if LaVonne hadn't insisted that I stop.

But I like the saneness of a grocery store. I like the structure of shoppers consulting their lists and checking off items one by one as they put them in their carts. I enjoy watching people who not only plan their lives but follow through on those plans. My mind, which is usually buzzing, flows slower in the market. Shopping is almost a meditation for me, as if, one by one, I am checking off my worries. LaVonne says I am the only person she knows who window-shops for food.

I was glad to be in the SuperValu, calming myself down. The events of the last two days had left me feeling under attack. I was deep in a near-Zen state, comparing cans of baked beans, when, out of the corner of my eye, I noticed a flash, a silver-streaked image. I tried to ignore it as I walked toward the end of the aisle, but at the end of canned fruit, it returned. Detective Brott was slinking back and forth between the aisles. I picked up a can of Chef Boyardee and began to read it, word-for-word. Five minutes later, he was still there.

"My god," I mumbled out loud to a jar of Prego, "he really does think I am involved with Bob's death. What else does he know about that night?"

I walked down the aisle toward canned soups and felt my knees buckle. My hands gripped the cart handle as I pushed it slowly toward the check-out line. My prison phobia was overtaking any sense of well-being I had left.

I looked around but Brott was gone. So was the joy of shopping.

"I'm originally from the south side of Chicago — where men are men and so are half the women." Lenny Milano, Noodles Comedy Club, Omaha, Nebraska.

7

Despite Bob's death, the police investigation, and my continued angst, happy hour continued as usual at The Comedy Box. The club's bar had always been popular with disillusioned office types who fancied themselves funny. They'd leave their nine-to-five drudgery and head to The Box where they'd down popular drinks like Sex on the Beach or Sand Up Your Tush and stare at photos of traveling comics that hung on the walls. Every bombed administrative assistant or marketing whiz would brag that they, too, if they gave up their day jobs, would become the next Lily Tomlin or Rodney Dangerfield.

At 4:10 on the day after my dinner with Lenny and LaVonne and eight hours after I caught Brott tailing me at the SuperValu, I found myself sitting on a barstool, feeling envious of my fellow road comics.

I longed to be working out-of-town. There's no better way to escape life than being a road comic. I'd be working a bar that featured comedy, Karoke and bad local bands. After the show I'd hang for one drink at the bar. A drunken Viet Nam vet would make a pass. I'd politely turn him down. I'd go back alone to my motel room. I'd get up the next morning and drive nine hours to another unimportant gig at another unknown dive. The only thing I'd have to worry about was whether the next motel would have HBO.

Instead, until I discovered who killed Bob, I had to stay in both Minneapolis and face the reality of life. There was no running away. And life for me at that moment waiting to talk to Dave and arguing with the bartender at The Box that Diet Cokes should be included in the happy hour two-for-one deal.

"Nothing doing, Mannie," Harry said. "Dave would fire me

if I gave away a free drink — even a Coke."

"Why do you work for him?" I asked.

"Why do you?" he snapped back.

"I have no choice," I answered, knowing that if I wanted to do comedy in Minnesota, I had to work for the man.

"Neither do I. I've got three kids at home," he said.

"Besides," the bartender smiled, "Dave's not that bad."

"He's not that good, either," I stated, trying to look hardened and bitter while sipping my Diet Coke out of a tiny bar straw.

"Are you here to schedule a booking? You haven't worked here in a while."

"My April has a few open dates," I told him, failing to mention that, except for my up-coming gig in Missouri, I was also open for the month of May, June, July and beyond. When it was boom time, comedians were booked two years in advance. Now we're lucky if we know where we'll be working next week.

"Did you know that Jimmie Walker is coming?"

"Get out of here! J.J. from "Good Times?"

"He's working the road as a stand-up."

"Wow. I'd love to be his opening act."

"You and everyone else in town."

We looked at each other and yelled Jimmy's trademark line, "Dyyyyyy-noooooo-mite!"

"Cut out the racket!" Dave screamed from the back.

"He must be off the phone," the bartender said.

"Wish me luck," I told him, sliding off the bar stool. "If I'm not out in a half-hour, send in reinforcements."

I put on my best John Wayne walk and headed back to Dave's office.

"You got a minute, Dave?" I asked as I leaned through his office doorway.

"Just one," Dave answered, not bothering to look up from his mound of paperwork. "The goddamn government. All I do is pay taxes and what do I get for it?"

"Freedom, roads, an education — oops, sorry, not that one."

"You're on awfully early," he grunted.

"Sorry, occupational hazard. It's been a weird couple of days."

"Tell me about it," Dave said, finally looking up at me. "I liked Bob."

"We all did," I said, saddened that the lump in my throat at the mention of Bob's name was becoming smaller with time. "I mean, I *really* liked him. Why else would I book him?" Dave asked with a look of bewilderment.

The fact that he would work for next to nothing crossed my mind.

"Speaking of booking," I said. Dave reached over and grabbed his calendar.

"I'm booked through February," he said.

"I've got a few weeks open in April," I told him as I sat down in the chair next to his desk. I suddenly remembered being in the same office just twenty-four hours earlier, being questioned by Detective Brott. Somehow the tiny room seemed bigger, now that it was only Dave and me. I could breathe in it.

"How many of your weeks are open?" Dave asked, bringing me back to the moment.

"All of them," I answered.

"You want the second week?"

"Sounds good. Usual price?"

"I've been meaning to talk to you about that," Dave said, once again averting his squinty little eyes from me.

"God, Dave, you pay half what other clubs pay now," I mumbled through tight lips.

"I need to cut back fifty bucks a week," he said, not even acknowledging my complaint.

"I'll take a cut of ten at the most," I told him.

"I'm going to be homeless one day because of you comics," Dave whined.

"You can always live in your Mercedes," I shot back.

"Mannie, sometimes I wonder why I book you at all."

"First of all, I'm cute as a button," I told him, knowing that flirting with any man, even Dave, usually works. For the first time since I entered his office, he almost smiled.

"And secondly, you know you can always count on me to do a good job."

One thing I know about my act — I'm consistent. I never

call in sick, am always on time and, most importantly, am always funny.

"You are reliable," Dave said.

"Bob was also someone who could be counted on," I told him, finally getting to the real reason that I had dropped by. I felt the killer was connected to Dave, but I didn't know how. "Do you think Bob was the real target or could it have been someone else?"

Dave looked at me intensely before he mumbled, "I don't know, Mannie. Someone wanting Bob dead doesn't seem likely, does it?"

"No, it doesn't," I answered.

"Who do you think they were after?" Dave asked, staring me straight in the eye.

"You," I told him, staring right back at him.

"Who would want to kill me?" he asked with so much innocence that I actually believed he was sincere.

"Do you mean besides everyone who's ever worked for you?" I asked incredulously.

"You know, Mannie," Dave responded, "for a woman, you've got really big balls."

I wanted to tell him that for a man he didn't, but I restrained myself. This was one pissing contest I didn't need to win. If Dave was involved, I needed to find out fast.

"Look, Dave, you must know you're not the most beloved club owner in the business."

"That's maybe true," he said, "but then I'm not the most hated, either."

I agreed with him on that. Some club owners make Sadam Hussein look like Billy Graham.

"Look, Mannie, I know that every time I refuse to book a comic, he or she hates me. That's the name of the game. And the ones I do book hate me because they claim I don't pay them enough."

"You don't," I told him, using the opportunity to remind him what a cheap bastard he was.

"You think I'm cheap because you're a comic. If you were a club owner, you'd think differently. I have money problems you

40

wouldn't begin to understand."

I started to wonder if Dave's self-proclaimed financial woes were real. That alone could make him a target.

"What kind of problems?" I asked, knowing I was stepping out of bounds, but I had no other choice.

"That's none of your business," he answered.

"Right now anything connected to Bob's death is my business. I paused before I made my confession. "Brott is convinced I'm involved."

"You?"

"Yep."

"Are you?" Dave asked, as he placed his hand on the handle of the side drawer of his desk. I suddenly remembered the old rumor that he kept a loaded semi-automatic in it.

"Jesus Christ, Dave, talk about the size of balls. Yours just doubled!" I watched as Dave pulled a threatening piece of Wrigley's Spearmint gum out of his drawer.

Dave actually smiled as he took my insult about his little buddies as a compliment. I didn't tell him that, even doubled, his balls were probably still smaller than green peas.

"Yeah, I killed him," I snarled at Dave, suddenly impatient to leave. "I was also on the grassy knoll in Dallas in '63."

"Hey, Brott's the one who thinks you're guilty, not me," Dave said gruffly, though I thought I detected a glimmer of sympathy. He unwrapped the gum and started to chew.

"Then you'll help me find the killer?" I asked, desperate to enlist everyone's help.

"I don't see how I can," he said.

"I want you to make a list of everyone who might want to knock you off," I told him, pushing a sheet of paper over for him to start writing.

Dave looked at the sheet of paper and laughed.

"Look around you, Mannie," he said, nodding at the thousands of photos that were scattered around the room. "Where do I begin?"

"I love entertaining at corporate events. I say a few things, get a thank you note and a big check. And the things I say are exactly the same things I used to say that would get me fired!"
Mannie Grand, Net World employee party.

8

Dave was adamant that no comic had it in for him enough to want him really dead. And I had to reluctantly agree. He claimed his life revolved around the club and that he was there sixteen hours a day. When I told him that Bob's last word was "Mannie" he seemed genuinely surprised.

I was afraid that Brott or Lenny had been telling what Bob had said. I didn't want rumors of my being a suspect spread around the comedy community. No one would hire a suspected murderer.

I needed every job I could get, especially the one I headed to after I left Dave's office. It was an exceptionally well-paying gig. Four hundred dollars for sixty minutes of work.

Occasionally I was blessed with what we comedians call "a corporate." A corporate is usually an employee party or a women's club special event. The pay is decent and the occasional ones I get keep me from drowning in debt.

I'm hired by corporations because, unlike a lot of comedians, I do a clean comedy act. I grew up watching Red Skelton and Lucille Ball. Since my act is traditional one-liners, performed rapid style, one after another, I'm often introduced as a female Rodney Dangerfield. I talk about being overweight and single, living with a roommate, driving a junker, being poor, dealing with creditors, and all the stuff that would mortally depress me if I didn't laugh about it. I occasionally throw in a political reference or a pseudo-intellectual jibe just to let people know I'm somewhat intelligent. But I find that most people, in clubs and the corporate world, would rather not think too much.

The corporate party I was working was being held in a

Holiday Inn banquet room. I waited patiently in the hallway of the hotel, going over my notes. The CEO's secretary had given me a ton of dirt about her boss, and I had to throw out ninety percent of it. She may have wanted to get fired, but I didn't.

The company was one of the many successful Minnesota computer businesses that kept the state solvent. The cars in the parking lot were Mercedes and Volvos. I should have bargained for more money.

Four hundred sounded like a lot of money to ask for a night's work, but it was a Saturday night, and I hadn't had any other work that week, or the week before. Besides, the paycheck covered more than a one-hour performance. It covered countless hours of practice and innumerable moments of despair.

An executive that I had been introduced to earlier leaned out of the banquet room doorway. "It will be a couple more minutes," he announced, and then asked with a chuckle, "Are you nervous?"

"I'm fine," I lied.

I've been asked that question a thousand times. Everyone wants me admit that I'm petrified and feel like throwing up. But I always lie and say, "I'm fine."

I wasn't fine. I was petrified and felt like throwing up. Before every show, I ask myself the same question: Why am I doing comedy? I, who at one time wanted to be a cop. Should I get a real job with real benefits? I could work security at WalMart. People don't get stage fright in housewares.

If I could have canceled the performance, I would have, but I needed the money too badly. Still, I was having difficulty focusing on my act.

Slowly, another thought crept up. I kept trying to push it back down because I needed to concentrate. But, if I wasn't the murderer, who was? And who was the murderer after? Was it Bob or LaVonne? Kenny? Grant Cuddler? Would another comedian, or even two, die before the case was solved?

I started to doodle Bob's face and name over my performance notes. Bob was 49 years old, eight years older than I. I knew there was a good chance that I would end up like Bob: single, broke and dead, with my obituary saying "survived by no one." There would be nothing in my obit except the year I was born and the year I died. My time on earth would be symbolized only by the lonely dash between birth and death.

My spirit was fading and I had to shape myself up and focus on the show I was about to do. My problems were mine alone, I kept reminding myself. This crowd didn't pay to see a loser.

I prayed the show would be good. It was always horrible to bomb at a private gig. At least in a club there would always be the chance I could redeem myself with the next show. In a corporate, I would walk out knowing there would be no second chance. For weeks, I'd be the conversation around the water cooler. "Boy, did that comic suck!"

I was going over my notes when something caught my attention. Hesitantly, I turned. Detective Brott was at the front desk. I stopped breathing for so long that I had to remind myself to start again. "Breathe, Mannie, breathe. It's only a detective — not the Grim Reaper." I looked at the door leading to the banquet room. The marketing guy would open it at any second. Brott was walking toward me.

The door opened and the company stiff leaned out and said, "We're ready for you."

I looked at Brott. He nodded at me to go into the banquet.

I trembled so much that as I walked toward the executive he laughed and said, "You lied to me. You are afraid!"

"More than you can imagine," I told him.

Fifty minutes and one mediocre performance later, I left the banquet room, Brott was gone.

"Boy, did that comic suck!" Fred the file clerk, after Mannie Grand's performance at Net World's employee party.

9

As I drove to meet LaVonne at The Box, after my corporate gig, I ruminated on the various ways I was going down for Bob's murder. If Brott had shown up just to unnerve me, it worked.

Playing on the movie screen inside my head was a 1939 black and white detective flick starring Humphrey Bogart. I didn't even star in my own fantasies. Bogie was wearing his trademark trenchcoat and fedora, but his face was Brott's. Although the cigarette that dangled from his mouth was unlit, smoke circled both the ceiling and my face. He leaned over his desk and told me matter-of-factly, "You're frying, Grand. You're frying for the murder of Bob Patterson."

"I'm innocent," I screamed. "Innocent!"

"That's what they all say," he smirked.

The credits rolled. Casting by Roseanne. Catering by Lean Cuisine.

The fantasy continued as I pulled into The Box's crowded parking lot. LaVonne and I had planned to go out to eat after her last set. Both performances had been sold out. Murder was good for business. It seemed like everyone in the Twin Cities wanted to visit the scene of the crime.

Three cop cars were parked outside the club. When I walked in, I noticed several armed policemen in the audience. Dave was taking no chances that history would repeat itself.

Grant Cuddler was on the stage and the audience was howling. He was well into his classic bit about Amish drag racers. Even I started to laugh.

I had never met Cuddler, but I owned the only comedy tape he had ever made. As a young comic, I must have watched it a hundred times. If anyone knows about the importance of timing, it's Grant Cuddler.

Sitting comfortably on a straight chair, his long legs stretched out in front of him, Grant smiled that glorious smile of his. He was the picture of contentment. His muscular arms were folded behind his head and his presence was warm and inviting. He appeared to be one of the nicest guys on the face of the earth. There was no way you'd ever guess he was one of the biggest jerks in the industry.

"He's amazing," I said to Dave, who was standing near me. Two days earlier a man had died on that stage, and Grant's professionalism erased, at least temporarily, any memory of it.

"He sure is. It's standing room only. What a great week," Dave said. For the first time since I'd known him, Dave was giddy with glee. I headed backstage.

A policeman stood outside the dressing room door and nodded at me as I went in. He didn't bother to ask my name. I could tell he knew who I was.

Yet I was glad to see the policeman hanging around backstage. If necessary, he could protect LaVonne.

LaVonne was sitting on the dressing room couch thumbing through Entertainment Today. Unlike a lot of comics, she never leaves before the end of the show.

"How was your corporate?" she asked as I closed the door.

"Sucked," I answered, as I flopped down on the couch next to her.

"How come?"

"Brott showed up."

"Jesus. Do you really think he suspects you?" she asked.

"Why else would he be there?" I asked. I hadn't told her about his stalking me at the SuperValu. I didn't want her worrying any more than she was already.

"Maybe he's got the hots for you."

"Not unless he's a psycho," I told her, "and with my luck, he probably is."

"Maybe it was just a coincidence."

"Not in a million years," I said, preferring to think that the crap in my life wasn't a product of random chaos.

"Wow, just like I predicted once in my first card-reading.

You have prison karma." LaVonne said, almost thrilled at her recollection. "Hey, maybe I should read Tarot for a living? What do you think?"

"I think I don't want to think about it."

"What are you going to do?" she asked.

"I only have one choice — solve the investigation myself," I told her.

"Can I help?" she asked. I knew she was sincere. LaVonne and I were classic best friends. There's nothing we wouldn't do for each other.

"I need all the help I can get," I said honestly. "I want to see what Grant knows. Can you get him to go out for coffee with us?"

"No problem. We just need to unbutton a few buttons and he'll agree to anything," she laughed. Even in the midst of the turmoil, Grant had been hitting on her. She wasn't attracted to him in the least.

LaVonne and I have different tastes in men. She likes nice, caring, intelligent men. I'm attracted to "bad boys" — those grown-up punks who think only of themselves. And, amazingly enough, a lot of bad boys are attracted to me.

Under different circumstances, Grant Cuddler would have been my cup of bitter tea.

"I was watching Grant perform," I told LaVonne. "He's remarkable."

"It's mind-boggling how he can be so cute and cuddly on-stage and such a creep off stage," she sighed.

"A lot of comics are like that. It's like they save all of their charm for the footlights. Is he really as nasty as they say?"

"I don't know if he's evil, but he's certainly not a joy," LaVonne paused, listening to Grant's monologue. He was talking about gambling on riverboats.

"This is his last bit," she said.

"Let's offer to buy him dinner. Have you ever known a comic to turn down a free meal?" I asked.

"Me," she answered.

"Besides you," I told her, noting a slight irritation on my part that she was disciplined and I wasn't.

"Mannie, sometimes I get the feeling that you don't like comedians," she said in all her naiveté.

"Just sometimes?" I laughed, amazed that this woman still wouldn't accept that I'm a born cynic. "LaVonne, in case you haven't noticed, I don't like a lot of things."

"Oh, you just get in funky moods," she said in an upbeat tone.

"For the last forty-one years?" I asked.

"You need more fiber," she responded.

One hour later I was sitting with LaVonne and Grant at Denny's. We only had to undo three buttons each to get Grant to come with us.

Grant was a tall, handsome, forty-something-year-old man. His classic jaw line jutted out like Mount Rushmore. He had hazel eyes and black wavy hair. His pumped-up biceps almost broke through his shirt-sleeves. He reminded me of the cover of a trashy romance novel.

I sat there imagining him on the cover, dressed in a pirate's outfit, though what he was wearing was pretty damn good. From his brown leather bomber jacket and white silk shirt to his neatly pressed pleated black pants, everything about him said success. The Rolex on his wrist must have cost fifteen grand.

Yet, I noticed that even with his "I've-got-the-world-by-its-coattail" image, he was more than agreeable to let me, dressed in my Lane Bryant clearance best, buy the Denny's Grand Slam breakfast.

LaVonne ordered an English muffin, dry, with a side order of fruit. I was submerged in the "Country Special" which featured eggs, biscuits, hash browns, sausage gravy and grits.

Our twentyish waitress sauntered over with more coffee. I noticed that Grant took in every inch of her with his eyes. Unlike the old days in comedy, no groupies hung out at The Box. On this tour, Grant had to find his own women.

"Thank you, darlin'," he said to the server in his deep baritone voice. "If you get a moment, stop by again and I'll give you a ticket to the show at The Comedy Box."

"You're a comedian?" the waitress gasped.

"It's just a job," he said with practiced humility.

I was ready to gag. LaVonne was already doing so.

"Have I seen you on TV?" she asked wide-eyed.

"Well, maybe. That is, if you watch "The Tonight Show."

Now he wanted "The Tonight Show" credit.

LaVonne and I looked at each other. She rolled her eyes. I rolled mine in agreement. We had been in this situation a hundred times, watching male comics use the "wouldn't you like to sleep with someone famous?" ploy.

I've even tried that sexual con game myself. It was in a small town in Iowa and I was drinking at the local hot spot after a show. The bartender was the good looking, hunky farmer type. I envisioned him chewing on a piece of straw. Oddly enough, the straw looked like me.

I decided he was a cross between Tom Cruise and Harrison Ford. The Fuzzy Navels I had drunk were not only playing havoc with my eyesight but they also caused my brain pan to overflow.

Finally, after twenty minutes of lusting, I got up my nerve, leaned over the bar and said, "Did you know I'm a comedian? Someday you can tell your grandkids you slept with a star."

The bartender leaned over and whispered, "Why would I tell them I slept with a Roseanne wanna-be?"

I haven't tried to pick up a man since.

"I do like you Northern women," Grant said as he watched the waitress wiggle away. He was being overly charming, almost to the point of ingratiating, and I was beginning to wonder why. Everything he said, as nicely worded as it was, was done through a tense little smile.

"Where are you from?" I asked Grant nonchalantly.

"Vegas," he answered. "I have a condo on the strip."

"You were born in Vegas?" I asked, always surprised that someone could actually be a native of that neon Mecca.

"I was born in Seattle," he responded. "I've lived in Vegas for twenty years. It's a great town."

"I've never understood why anyone from a warm climate would travel to Minnesota in the winter," I told him as we both watched LaVonne add a half cup of cream to her coffee.

He gave me a "none of your damn business" look, and shrugged his shoulders.

"These days you've got to go where the work is," LaVonne said in a tone of voice that was meant to remind me that we were trying to become Grant's friends, not his enemies, at least until we found out if he killed Bob.

"You've got that right, pumpkin," Grant smiled at her as he pulled out a cigar and lit it.

"I bet you'll never forget this week," I stated with all the tact of an army tank driving through a Baskin Robbins.

"This week's been shit," he said. "I'd like to get the hell back to Vegas, but Dave won't let me out of the contract."

"The murder's been great for the numbers at the club," I told him. "It's been a sell-out crowd every night. Everyone wants to come to the scene of the crime"

Grant grunted in a low tone, "Some of them could be coming to see me."

"I only meant..." I began to stammer, realizing how overly sensitive Grant was. I would have to watch every word I said to him. His arrogance was beginning to look more and more like a cover-up for insecurity. Maybe he was an okay guy after all.

Warning lights started going off in my head. Big time. I'd been there before, making excuses for some jerk and thinking all along that underneath his crappy exterior he was goodness personified. It never turned out that way. Beneath their crappy exteriors was more crap. But by the time I found out, it was too late. By then I was hopelessly hooked.

"Bob was such a great guy," LaVonne interjected, helping me out.

"I'm sure he was," Grant agreed, his eyes focused on the waitress's backside that was conveniently bent over a table in front of ours. He inhaled deeply on the stogie in his mouth and I doubted that it was the cigar he was thinking of.

"You never met Bob before?" LaVonne asked, obviously trying to get his attention back to the two of us.

"Bob was always on the road," I pitched in. "He loved to travel. One time he had a gig in Alaska. He was too terrified to fly so he went by Greyhound instead. It took him five days. The ticket was three hundred and five dollars. His salary was three hundred. Bob always bragged that it only cost five bucks to see Anchorage."

LaVonne laughed a little too loudly at that and Grant turned away from admiring the restaurant's featured buns to look at LaVonne as she added, "That's why we thought the two of you might have known each other before. Bob was a true road warrior."

"Darlin', I've worked with thousands of comics," Grant sighed. "I can't remember who I worked with last month let alone who I've met over the years. Why would I bother to remember anyone else on the show?"

LaVonne dropped her fork. Her perkiness instantly froze into ice princess. Grant felt the deep freeze wafting across the table.

"I didn't mean you, sweetie," he said in a voice that managed to be both patronizing and chauvinistic. "I'll always remember you. You're special."

LaVonne opened her mouth to speak and was a nanosecond away from chastising him when I kicked her under the table.

"Ow!" was all she said.

"I can't believe the bars close at 1:00 a.m. in this town," Grant complained loudly, his smoky eyes crinkling in disgust.

I never knew how sexy a grump could be.

"I'm glad they close early," I told him, sticking up for my frozen tundra. "It makes the streets a little safer."

"But I'm wide awake and there's nothing to do," he whined as he put his cigar in the ashtray and then reached over and grabbed both of our hands. With his thumbs he started making small circles on our palms. "Well, maybe one thing..."

It was easy to tell what he was thinking. LaVonne and I are often approached by horny male comics who try to seduce us into a me*nage-a-trois*. I've never understood men's fascination or logic in their quest for a sexual three-way. Why do they think they can pleasure two women when they have enough difficulty pleasuring one? Sometimes I think that the higher the

51

testosterone count, the lower the number of brain cells.

"Let's go bowling!" LaVonne abruptly suggested while quickly pulling back her hand. "The Stardust is open twenty-four hours."

"Sounds great!" I responded.

"How about going back to my room?" Grant offered. He was tenacious.

"We'd rather bowl," I mumbled, as LaVonne yanked my hand back from Grant's, something I had failed to do myself. Anything to help the investigation, I lied to myself.

"My room is nice and cozy," Grant whispered, looking directly into my eyes. By now he could probably tell he had no chance with LaVonne.

Why did the bastard think he could easily bed me?

"Because," the annoying devil that often sits on my well-padded shoulders responded, "not only could he, but more than likely, someday, would."

"Dammit," I replied out loud and both LaVonne and Grant looked at me. I smiled weakly.

"What about the casino?" LaVonne asked, not bothering to ask why I swore. She knew me well enough to know when I was going into hormone overdrive. She also knew me well enough to know I'd never go to Mystic Lake. Why was she bringing it up?

"Mystic Lake Casino is open twenty-four hours," she smiled, giving me the he'll-never-fall-for-it-anyway-look, and added an if-he-does-I'll-keep-an-eye-on-you-and-your-gambling look.

After people live together for so many years, they have more looks than dialogue.

"I live in Vegas. Why would I gamble at your rinky-dink casino?" Grant smirked.

"Hey, our casinos are as good as any in Vegas. Mystic Lake has at least two thousand slots," I shot back, surprised that I was sticking up for a place that had cost me at least twenty thousand dollars since it opened.

"They also have blackjack and bingo," LaVonne said. I was amazed at her knowledge. As far as I knew, she had never stepped foot in the place.

"Bingo? What am I? A blue-haired old lady? I'm sorry, but

gambling in this state is for losers," Grant responded.

I thought of my Dad. I thought of me. I thought of the hundreds of people I had met in G.A.

"Are you against gambling?" I asked, wondering at his sudden high-handed moral tone that had, ironically, followed his offer of sexual perversion.

Grant's eyes darkened.

"I gamble," he stated firmly. "But your casinos have a hundred-dollar betting limit."

"Grant, that means you can only bet a hundred a bid," I told him, in case he didn't know. "A hand takes what? Two minutes to play? Theoretically, you could lose three thousand bucks an hour."

"That's what I mean," he said as he snuffed out his cigar. "Minnesota gambling is for kids."

"The last time I was in Las Vegas I took thousands of dollars out of one machine. Unfortunately, it was an ATM." Mannie Grand, on-stage at Kopitzke's Cheese and Chew, Hudson, Wisconsin.

10

It was 3:30 a.m. when we dropped Grant off at the condo and headed home. We had sat at Denny's until 3:00 talking business. It was the same-old same-old, complaining about who was funny and who wasn't, and reminiscing about the good old days.

In the last two weeks I had heard of three comics, all of them headliners with national television credits like A&E at The Improv and The Dave Letterman Show, who had left the business and taken full-time jobs. One became a used car salesman, another a bill collector, and the third was a born-again who entered a seminary. They had all tired of living-the-lie that someday they'd make it big.

After we dropped Grant off, both LaVonne and I were too anxious to fall asleep. Until I found the killer, my future as a free woman was still in question. LaVonne decided to do a Tarot reading as soon we got home.

I decided to use a different tactic to ease my anxiety — freshman logic. I stopped at the Mini Mart and bought a red spiral notebook. As soon as we walked into the apartment, I sat at the kitchen table and wrote "POTENTIAL SUSPECTS" across the front cover. The only way I knew to solve this murder was to treat it like the exercises I had done in Criminology 101. I hoped this project, like my earlier college projects, would earn an "A."

"Am I a suspect?" LaVonne asked, as she sat across from me.

"Everyone is a potential suspect, including you." I smiled, knowing she doesn't even kill mosquitoes. She catches them in an aquarium net and carries them outside to freedom.

"And my motive would be?" she asked, taking the cards out of a purple velvet bag. She placed her "How To Read The Tarot" instruction booklet next to the stack. I glanced at the publisher's name and address. It was not comforting to note that the supposed blueprint for my future was printed in Taiwan.

I had purchased the colorful cards for her at WalMart on Christmas Eve. I bought them because they were on sale. No other reason. It was either the Tarot cards or Monopoly. Too bad I didn't give her the latter; I could have used a get-out-of-jail-free card.

"I haven't listed motives yet," I told her, as I opened the notebook. "First I need to make a list of everyone's good and bad traits."

"Tell me my bad traits," LaVonne begged.

"Don't you want to know your good ones?" I asked her, amazed how she can always lighten the moment.

"I already know those," she bragged.

"Then tell me 'cause I'm having a hard time coming up with any," I teased.

"I'm very honest. I perform at the Toys for Tots benefit every year and I never gossip unless it's too juicy not to."

"I have gossip under your bad column."

"You do not!" she laughed.

"Yes, I do."

I held up the notebook so LaVonne could see the list.

"Guess I'd better watch my tongue," she laughed. "Anything else horrendous about me?"

"Nothing, except that you'd run a psychic hotline from our apartment if I'd let you."

"At least mine would be legit," she protested.

"You cannot tell the future," I reminded her.

"I knew you'd say that," she shot back, triumphant.

I put down my notebook. I wasn't comfortable with what I was going to say. I wanted to be wrong. I wanted the murderer to be a stranger, a nut case with no reason to kill Bob or anyone else. That, as crazy as it sounds, would be comforting to me.

"Grant's the heavy so far. After that, it's Dave or Lenny," I told her.

"Or just some wacko in the audience," LaVonne said, reminding me of that slight possibility. "Do you want me to start the Tarot reading now?"

"No," I answered.

As usual, she didn't listen.

"I am now laying down the Significator," LaVonne said, her voice colored with an exaggerated eeriness.

"What are you talking about?" I asked, still not used to all the New Age lingo she often used.

"The Significator is the card that represents you," she told me as she held it up.

I saw that it was a picture of a queen.

"Royalty, that's cool. I assume I'm a queen because I'm noble," I said, thinking that for once she was on the right track.

"Nope," LaVonne replied. "It's because you're old — over forty. If I were laying down the Significator card that represented me, it would be the card with a picture of a youthful page on it because I am young and under forty."

"You're thirty-nine," I told her.

"According to the booklet, forty's the cut-off age for being either old or young. You're also the Queen of Pentacles because you have dark hair and eyes."

"And you think this is scientific?" I asked her, awed that someone so intelligent could be sucked into such paranormal bullshit.

"Extremely," she answered.

I shook my head in disbelief and returned to my list as LaVonne continued with otherworld mumbo-jumbo. I only hoped I'd never come home and find our crockpot filled with frogs' feet and eyes of newt.

"What do you think are Lenny's bad traits?" I asked her, hoping to get her off her psychic joy ride.

"Why is Lenny a suspect? They were best friends."

"I'm just making a list of potential suspects. I'm not saying he did it. Come on, what are his vices?"

"Small ones, I guess. Stealing."

"Money?"

"Material. His line, 'Why doesn't a complimentary beverage

tell you what a fine person you are?' is George Carlin's bit."

"Do you think Lenny gambles?"

"Not that I know of. Sometimes he drinks too much."

"He always drinks too much. What about sex scandals?"

"God, Lenny blushes if you even mention a woman to him," LaVonne said. "Wait a minute. I did hear he was kicked out of a strip joint in Sioux Falls. He was there with a few other comics and he became pretty obnoxious. He kept screaming 'I want a woman! Why can't I have a woman?'"

"That doesn't sound like him. Was he on drugs?"

"Not that I know of, but then nobody who does drugs tells me. I make my anti-drug stance fairly well known. I do know of a few that partake — Jimmy Foltz, Chris Burn, Milos — all those guys are into coke."

"I thought Milos was in recovery."

"He's in and out."

"I wasn't even thinking about putting Milos on the list."

"I don't think Milos is involved. He's actually kind of sweet."

"Not sweet enough," I told her, remembering the nights of lukewarm passion that she and Milos had shared.

"He just wasn't my type," she sighed.

"As I recall, you were certainly his," I reminded her.

"That's true." she answered and dropped it at that. Being the object of lust was hardly new for LaVonne.

"Are we going to spend all night making lists or can I tell you what the Tarot cards predict?" she asked as she studied the cards.

"Let me finish Dave Olson's list first."

"You'll need another notebook just for his bad traits."

"He's cheap," I began, knowing we could go on all night with the club owner's faults.

"An asshole," LaVonne responded.

"A liar," I told her, remembering how he was constantly caught lying about salaries.

"Then why do we like him?" she asked with a slight smile.

"I have no idea," I answered, realizing that a small part of me, a very small part, liked Dave. "There's just something about the guy, though I think 'like' is stretching it a bit. Is there anything bad about Dave that I don't already know?"

"Did you know he once did time?" she said, dropping her bomb nonchalantly.

I immediately started erasing in my notebook.

"What are you doing?" LaVonne asked.

"I'm moving the word 'gossip' from your bad list to your good one."

LaVonne smiled. "See? Sometimes it's good to know stuff about other people."

LaVonne placed the final cards on the table in front of her. She'd look at a card and then turn to her book, look at another and repeat the same action. As she turned over the last card, her smile quickly disappeared. She put one hand over her mouth and with the other hand reached over and grabbed mine.

"I'm so sorry," she mumbled.

"What is it?" I asked, trying not to give credence to her store-bought predictions. My gut was telling me, however, to listen.

"I'm so sorry," she repeated over and over.

"I do not believe at all in this ridiculous game," I told her, angry that once again she had suckered me in. "But if you do not tell me what you see in that stupid card, I will never talk to you again."

"The last card I laid down represents the future," she said, keeping her hand placed on top of it.

I carefully lifted her hand. The card was turned upside-down but I could see it was a white horse with a rider. The rider was a skeleton and wore a suit of armor. The horse it was riding on was stepping over decaying carcasses.

The title of the card was a simple one.

"DEATH."

"Hundreds attended the memorial service for slain funny man, Bob Patterson. At the end of the service, everyone was given a tiny rubber chicken key chain. PJ, columnist, *Minneapolis Star & Tribune.*

1 1

The ritual of a funeral confuses me as much as death itself. I envy the societies that encourage wailing and gnashing of teeth at the death of a loved one. Straightforward outright grief seems more natural than western civilization's stoic acceptance and then party-like wake.

As we sat politely in the chapel of the oldest church in Minneapolis, it seemed ironic to me that the Reverend Tom Clay was telling us Bob's funeral would be "a celebration."

I looked at the long box holding Bob. The undertaker had dressed him in a polyester suit that will undoubtedly last longer than the carefully embalmed body.

I turned my head slowly and realized that there were no family members mourning Bob. I recognized every sad face in the somber crowd. There were no strangers lurking about. I've read enough mystery novels that I knew there was a good chance that, like a proud artist at a gallery opening, the killer could be in the room,

I looked again at the dark maroon casket and too few funeral wreaths that were sent by other jokesmiths. The one from LaVonne and me was the second biggest. The largest, surprisingly, came from Grant.

I looked at Detective Brott who was seated in a pew. His eyes were on me, not the minister. I did not feel like celebrating. I wanted, instead, to wail.

Reverend Tom requested a moment of silence. He told us that we should meditate on Bob's life as we listened to a tape of Bob's favorite song. I wondered if the good minister bothered to check out the music beforehand. When the music began, I realized he hadn't.

Both LaVonne and I started to giggle and then, like everyone else, broke into laughter. In the holiest of places, "Dancin' In The Streets" by Martha and the VanDellas reached the rafters. By the end of the song everyone in the church was singing, swaying, and clapping their hands to the music.

It was a celebration of Bob's life after all.

"Peace be with you," Reverend Tom said, quietly ending the service.

"That's that," LaVonne sighed, standing up and straightening her blue and white flowered dress. It was a dress that was designed to be large and baggy. It was her "cute orphan" look. Earlier, I had put on a similar dress, except on me the fit was too tight. I changed into a black pantsuit and white turtleneck, not noticing until I left home that I looked like a priest. We looked like a remake of "Boys Town."

"It was a nice service after all," I said to LaVonne. I hate clichéd situations where I can think of nothing to say except an even more clichéd remark.

"Martha and the VanDellas were a great addition."

"They always are," I answered, knowing that one of my many regrets in life is that I was never a Motown singer, even though I can't carry a tune or even one note. R&B is one of my passions. I am completely devoted to Gladys Knight. I would kill to be one of her Pips. And don't even mention Aretha Franklin to me, or I break out in tears.

"Nice service," Detective Brott said as he walked up to us. "How's it going, Mannie?"

"I'm doing okay," I told him, wondering if Brott would ever leave me alone. "I'll miss Bob."

I looked up and it seemed that although Brott wasn't smiling at me, his eyes certainly were. His demeanor toward me was gruff and coldly professional but there was a softness that once in a while showed through, whether he wanted it to or not. When he noticed how intensely I was looking at him, he turned to LaVonne and asked, "How's it going at the club this week?"

"It's sold out every night," she answered.

She didn't bother to add that he should already know the

answer to his question. The club had been swarming with cops.

"I caught your act. You're pretty funny," he said, as if he was surprised that a comic could be funny.

"Thanks. Getting laughs is always a plus in comedy," LaVonne said dryly.

"I hear that Bob wasn't very good," he told us in a voice loud enough to wake the dead — or, more specifically, Bob.

"Do we have to talk about him? I mean, he's just a few feet away," I said angrily, glancing back toward the casket.

"Sorry," Brott said, looking embarrassed that I caught him acting like a jerk. "Mannie, are you hanging around for a while?"

"I'm staying for the brunch," I told him, wanting to add that it was none of his business what I did.

"That's not what I mean," he said, pulling out a cigarette and placing it unlit between his lips. "I mean, do you plan on staying in town for a while?"

"A week or so," I told him, remembering my upcoming gig in Missouri.

"Do me a favor," he said, looking directly into my eyes, "don't leave town just yet. Stay until I tell you you can leave."

And with that, he walked off.

"Damn, damn, damn," I said to LaVonne, forgetting for a moment that I was in a place of worship. "I have to go to St. Louis. I have a contract. I need the money."

"Go talk to him. I think he'll listen to reason. I think he kind of likes you."

"Are you nuts?" I told her, knowing she mistakenly thinks every man is attracted to me like they are to her. "He hates me. He thinks I killed Bob."

"Ah, he just likes to play bad cop, bad cop," LaVonne said.

LaVonne and I headed to the church basement. We had reached the top of the steps when I said, "Wait here."

"Mannie," she said firmly, but this time it didn't work. She could tell where I was heading.

I had never been so angry in my life. I stomped over to Brott who was talking with Dave.

"Dave, can you please excuse us?" I almost spit the words out. Dave quickly retreated across the room.

I knew no one could hear what I said to Brott, but everyone was watching.

"Listen, you, I didn't kill Bob."

"I didn't say you did," Brott said to me, showing absolutely no emotion.

"Did you ever think that maybe his last word was 'Mannie' because we were friends? You want to find the murderer? Then look somewhere else. You're wasting valuable time trying to pin it on me."

"I'm not trying to pin anything on anyone," Brott said, clearly irritated. "I'm just doing my job."

"Ha!" I said, as I walked away, wishing I had a better comeback than "Ha!" I'd think of a thousand retorts later and would wish I had used every one.

I joined LaVonne as she stared at me, opened-mouthed, from the stairwell. We headed to the basement in silence.

Dave had footed the bill for a lunch made by the church's Ladies Auxiliary. By the time we reached the bottom of the steps, there was already a long line at the buffet table.

LaVonne and I walked to the back of the line. The school of thought that suggested telling someone off to make yourself feel better was, I decided, bullshit. I felt decidedly worse. I looked around the basement and noticed where all the windows and exits were. There were too many people, too many cops. My claustrophobia was setting in.

"The food looks wonderful," she said to me, directing my attention to the much needed diversion.

The good women of the church had made dozens of hotdishes, including my favorite — green beans drowning in mushroom soup and topped with fried onion rings. There were wiggly molds of lime green Jell-O dotted with miniature marshmallows. Homemade breads and muffins were still steaming from the oven. At the end of the table, small squares of white cake with candied lemon slices beckoned to me.

"I should go to church more often," I told LaVonne, forgetting my fears as I piled my plate as high as possible. I would feel great by the end of the line.

The Kid walked up to us as I was trying to fit a piece of cake on the edge of my plate.

"You guys want to sit with us?" he asked.

"Sure," I said, as the cake toppled off the mountain of food on my plate. The Kid caught it in mid-air.

"We're in the corner." The Kid pointed toward the table where Milos The Magnificent was sitting alone.

"Did you take off work to come to the funeral?" I asked as we walked toward Milos.

"What work? I was laid off by the coffee house."

"Why? Gathering Grounds is such a popular place."

"That's the problem. It's so popular two more shops just like it opened on the same block."

The Kid didn't seem worried about his lack of employment. At 18 he assumed that time was sitting in a bottle, waiting for him to open and use it at will.

He was right. Even if he did comedy for ten years before he made it big, he'd only be 28. In that same ten years, I'd be in my fifties and planning to retire on an unfixed and unfixable income.

"Can you believe this spread?" I asked, jumping into small talk so that no one would notice how nervous I was.

"I'm glad Charley's Deli didn't cater it," The Kid laughed crudely.

"Hey, Charley was Bob's friend, too," I reminded him. In fact, I was surprised that Charley wasn't at the service. Perhaps he wanted to avoid any finger pointing and whispered comments.

We sat down at the table. LaVonne said a brief hello to Milos. He nodded in return and went back to looking at his food.

"It's hard to believe Dave's footing the bill for this," LaVonne said as she dug into a tater-tot hotdish.

"He had no choice," The Kid said.

"What do you mean?" I asked.

"I figure Dave owes it to Bob. I think the killer was really after Dave," The Kid said bluntly.

"I think so, too," Milos The Magnificent added, while twirling the food on his plate. Milos seemed to eat only for survival while I seem to survive only to eat.

Milos was a few years younger than me, yet treated me like I was a senior citizen. I could never tell if it was out of respect or disdain.

Like a lot of people his age, he's into what he calls "body art." I just call them tattoos. I could see at least five running up his hands and arms. LaVonne has assured me there are many more.

"Everybody wants Dave dead," Milos The Magnificent said as he put down his fork and pulled a cigarette out of his front pocket. As soon as he lit it, a church lady quickly ran over and told him to put it out.

There were two bad things about Milos The Magnificent — the first was that he reeked of stale cigarettes, and the second was that he was not even close to being magnificent. He was a mediocre magician at best, but he liked his self-imposed title and we all went along with it.

Milos performed comedy-magic, meaning he told old jokes and did old tricks, like putting a glass bottle in a brown paper bag and crumpling the bag into a little ball. The disappearing bottle trick can be bought at any magic shop for $29.95. For his finale, instead of pulling a rabbit out of a hat, he pulled a hat out of a rabbit.

"Wanting someone dead is a far cry from committing a murder," I said as I reached for the salt. "Besides, I don't think anybody actually wants to see Dave dead."

"Just unconscious for a while," LaVonne added. Then, she lowered her head and whispered sarcastically, "Look who decided to bless us with his presence."

I turned and saw that Grant Cuddler had walked into the room. I also noticed Milos glaring at Grant. I wondered if he was jealous of Grant's talent or jealous that LaVonne and Grant were working together for the week.

Milos still had it bad for LaVonne. But then, most of the men she dated and dropped did. She's not an easy person to forget.

Everyone in the room turned and looked at the late-arriving Cuddler. Grant's hair was uncombed and his clothes were wrinkled. He looked as if he had just gotten out of bed. For him, that's a good look.

He walked straight to Dave's table. They shook hands and Grant handed his coat to Dave. Dave took it and hung it up.

Grant then talked with Brott for a few minutes. He and Brott turned and looked at our table. Grant gave us a half-wave. I could tell he was going to join us, and I was surprised. I assumed he would sit with Dave. Most comedians continually kiss-up to the club owner.

I watched Grant go through the food line. He carefully picked out each item while charming the church ladies in the process. Grant had a thing for women who served him.

"My alarm clock didn't go off," Grant announced as he sat down at our table.

Grant was staying at the comedy condo. Most of the clubs purchase condos to house out-of-town comics. The condos are cheaper than motels and an equity-generating investment for the club owner. For the comedians, the condos had the distinct disadvantage of little, if any, housekeeping. Week after week, comedians who party hard, smoke a lot, and have sex with as many partners as they can, rarely remember to clean up after themselves. The rule of thumb when staying in a comedy condo is to bring your own sheets and a bottle of Lysol.

"The flowers you sent were beautiful," I told Grant. He looked uncomfortable that I mentioned them.

A long silence followed until The Kid blurted out, "Milos was just saying that the killer was probably after Dave." The Kid reiterated his little theory while balancing a spoon on the end of his nose.

"Makes perfect sense to me," Grant answered.

"Dave called us at eight a.m. to make sure we were coming," LaVonne told everyone at the table.

"Same here," said Milos. The Kid nodded in agreement.

At the same time, all of us turned and looked at Dave who was talking non-stop to Brott.

"Well," I said, "I wonder if it's Dave who wanted all of us here or..."

"The cops," LaVonne finished.

"God, what a pain in the ass this whole thing is," Grant groaned. "I knew I should never have taken a two-week gig in Minnesota."

"It must be wild to go on-stage knowing that there could be

a killer in the house," The Kid said, chatty as ever, as if he were talking about going to a movie or the latest baseball scores.

"Damn right," Grant said, digging into his food.

I love watching a man who loves to eat.

"Maybe the killer wasn't an audience member," The Kid said. "Maybe the killer was someone backstage — like LaVonne."

"Yeah, sure," LaVonne said, showing him how long her middle finger was. "Just now, while your head was turned, I slipped poisoned mushrooms into that tuna and noodle thing you're eating."

The Kid looked at his plate and started to push it away and then laughed and started eating it again.

"I know you're not the killer," he stated flatly.

"And why is that?" LaVonne asked. She acted bored with his ever-present teenage insolence.

"Well, first of all, the killer has to be very intelligent!"

LaVonne threw a hard roll at The Kid's head and managed to score a perfect shot right in the middle of his forehead. It bounced off his head and The Kid caught it and took a bite out of it.

"And, of course, he had to be very quick," The Kid continued.

"Diversity, please!" LaVonne demanded.

"Sorry. He or she had to move like lightning," The Kid informed us. "Of course, if it was somebody backstage, like LaVonne, then agility wouldn't matter. Maybe she could have done it after all."

"Hey," LaVonne said, recognizing even a mild put-down when she heard it.

"LaVonne wasn't the only one who had access to backstage," I told The Kid. "Virtually everyone did. The door to the green room wasn't locked."

"I didn't think of that," The Kid said, dejected.

Is everyone trying to solve the murder? I asked myself. Do we all consider each other a suspect?

"We know that LaVonne, Lenny, Dave and Grant were backstage," I told them.

"Don't forget Bob and Charley," Grant added.

"Bob didn't kill himself and Charley wouldn't poison anyone," I told them. "At least not intentionally."

I knew the deli owner well. The last ten pounds I gained were a result of his seasoned French fries.

"There's always the best-friend angle." The Kid pointed out, animated again. "You said Lenny was backstage?"

"Only for a few minutes" LaVonne said, picking at her dessert.

"Hey, why isn't Lenny here?" The Kid asked, looking around.

"He's on the road," I told him. To a comic, paid work is an excuse to miss anything. Even your own funeral if you had to.

"You know, Mannie, I think the cops may have narrowed the list," Grant said quietly. "Turn around, slowly."

I glanced over my shoulder and Brott was staring directly at me. His arms were folded in front of him and he was frowning, big-time.

"Have you got a record we don't know about, Mannie?" The Kid laughed.

"I've never even had a speeding ticket," I told The Kid truthfully. "I'm nothing like the rest of my..."

I stopped, unable to finish my sentence because, just like in a cartoon, a light bulb exploded inside my head and I suddenly knew why Brott didn't trust me.

My bouncing baby brother. I didn't know how or why but somehow I was certain Chet had something to do with Bob's death.

"I'm in so many twelve-step groups that I have 144 steps I have to do. I just joined a new one. It's called Workaholics Anonymous. We meet about eight times a week." Mannie Grand, practicing in front of the mirror in her bathroom.

12

My dad still lived in our family house on Johnson Street in Northeast Minneapolis. It was a working class neighborhood of Swedes, Poles, Norwegians and a few American Mutts like me. The weekends were spent mowing yards or shoveling snow. The residents kept a respectable distance, knowing that good chain-link fences made good neighbors. They quietly watched out for each other. When they did talk, it was usually about the weather.

Weatherspeak is the second language of Minnesotans. Because we exist in a climate where sixty below wind-chill factor is not uncommon in the winter and summer temperatures can be in the nineties with eighty percent humidity, weather is an obsession. To my dad there are only three topics of conversation: the weather forecast, gambling, and more gambling.

Dad was sitting in his olive-green recliner, his dinner spread out in front of him on a TV tray that was covered in painted flowers and rust. My dinner was also on a tray. I was still full from stuffing myself five hours earlier at Bob's wake.

"It's gonna snow later this week," Dad said as we sat together watching the Weather Channel.

The furniture in the room hadn't been replaced in 17 years. Right before Mom died, she purchased the orange and yellow-flowered couch and the two green overstuffed armchairs the same day. The pole lamps, with their gold petal-shaped glass shades, probably looked good back then. The room, as garish as it was, would have been brighter had she lived longer.

"There's still a lot of winter left," I said as I wiped my mouth with a paper napkin.

"You betcha," Dad replied. He used his remote to click over to the local newscast. "You can have a blizzard in April."

"We usually have one around the state hockey tournament," I said, making small talk, the only kind Dad and I have. "I've got a couple of fish sticks left."

"Don't worry. I'll give 'em to the dog," he said.

My dad is in his seventies. Somewhere in his limited memory bank is the fact that at one time or other in my life, I loved pizza and fish sticks. Now, whenever I show up, he serves both.

"Your friends treating you good?" I asked. This was our code for 'Is anyone after you because you owe them money?'

"Everything's okay," he said, which meant "Not right now."

I breathed deeply and asked a question that I hadn't asked in years. "What do you hear from Chet these days?"

My dad looked up. I could tell he was wondering why I asked. Chet was a topic I normally refused to discuss.

"You know I hardly see Chet," Dad said, protective of his son, as usual. He believed everyone wanted to lock Chet away, including me.

I knew Chet had at least three outstanding warrants. But with limited jail capacity and over 31,000 outstanding warrants in Hennepin County, ranging from misdemeanors to felonies, unless it was murder, the police took a long time to find you.

"I need a favor," I said to Dad, watching him toss fish sticks to Halley, his aging German Shepherd. Dad named her after the comet because, as a puppy, she'd streak through a room. Now, like Dad, she creeps slowly across the floor.

"If you need money, I know of a sure thing in the fourth at Canterbury Downs. We could go in together. I could scrape up at least twenty," Dad said excitedly.

"You know I don't gamble anymore," I reminded him. "Actually, I need two favors. Do you still know some of the big players in Vegas?"

"A few."

"I need you to find out some information. There's a chance that a friend of mine's in trouble. I think he might owe money to the wrong people."

"I can do that. What else do you want?"

"I want to see Chet."

"Being in a family teaches us how to love — because there's no way you could ever like anyone you're related to." Mannie Grand, Minnesota State Fair, Comedy Stage.

13

I waited at a reading table in the library on Hennepin and 27th for my brother to arrive. There was always the chance that Chet would stand me up. Actually, when I thought about it, there was no reason for him to show. We were never close, not even as kids.

As a kid, Chet tore the heads off my Barbies, tormented my cat, and destroyed any game or book that was mine.

"He'll grow out of it," my mother always said. Even then I knew that her apathy toward Chet's psychotic behavior and dad's non-stop gambling had ruined me for any decent male/female relationship.

Because Mom worked full-time, I was the one who did all the cooking and cleaning. Chet was never required to do any chores. He was either a whirlwind, tearing up our house, or plopped in front of the TV as he watched "Gilligan's Island" while ingesting large quantities of Cocoa Puffs and orange soda.

He started getting into serious trouble when he was eleven. Chet's first heist was a Three Musketeers bar from the local Mini-Mart. He progressed to toys and watches at the mall. At 14, Chet came home with Christmas presents for all of us, direct from Dayton's department store. He gave Mom a pair of 14k gold earrings and Dad a leather wallet. I received a set of lobster forks—probably the only thing he could fit into his pocket at the time.

He claimed he bought the presents with money he earned shoveling sidewalks. My parents never challenged the fact that, to our knowledge, he had not shoveled a single walk. Instead of punishing him, my parents proudly showed their friends the gifts their loving son had given them.

I threw mine in the trash.

It was that same Christmas that I started attending the Twelfth Avenue Baptist Church. I, who had descended from a family of thieves and gamblers, decided religion was the only way I could rebel.

On Sunday mornings, as Dad read the racing news while Mom worked as a fry cook at a truck stop in Fridley and Chet roamed the malls, I stood in the front pew, choir book in hand, singing praises, loud and off-key, to the Lord.

And today, though I haven't been to church in a decade, I still find myself humming "Will the Circle be Unbroken?" from time to time. In fact, I was humming it when Chet walked up and tapped me on the shoulder.

"Sounds like you've still got the spirit," Chet said with a smug smile as he sat across from me.

"And I'm sure you don't," I responded sarcastically. I scrutinized Chet's appearance. He had changed so much that if he hadn't sat next to me, I would not have recognized him.

I had not seen him in nine years. He was at least a hundred pounds heavier. My mom's side of the family tends to be large. I, too, take after my Mom but Chet had taken that tendency to an extreme. At only five foot eight he had to be well over three hundred pounds. He sported a long beard that reached to the middle of his barrel chest. Just like his hair, his fingernails were caked with dirt.

He had something else I hadn't seen before, a scar running diagonally across his face.

I thought of our last family portrait, taken years ago at K-Mart. Chet was a teenager then. With his light brown hair and blue eyes, he looked like the eternal innocent. Looking at him now, though he was only thirty-eight years old, he looked fifty.

I remembered Oscar Wilde's line, "We all get the face we deserve in the end."

Chet's face looked like a death mask.

"So, how you doing?" I asked with more sincerity than I thought possible.

"Same old, same old," he responded. "I was surprised you wanted to see me. What's it been, ten years?"

"Nine," I answered, remembering the last time we were together. I had caught him stealing from Dad. He was going through the desk drawer where Dad hid the little money he had.

"I need something from you," I told him. I felt my heart almost clinch. I never thought I would be desperate enough to ask Chet for anything.

"Why in hell do you think that, after all these years, I would do anything for you?" he snarled.

"You owe me," I told him. "I'm the one who takes care of Dad. I'm the one who checks on him, shovels his snow, and keeps him from blowing his entire Social Security check at Bingo."

"You're supposed to be there for Dad. I don't owe you anything. You've never been there for me."

"I was there, Chet. You just expected me to be driving your get-away car," I told him, staring him straight in the eyes, determined not to let him intimidate me ever again.

"I'm in trouble, Chet," I said quietly, my eyes suddenly filling with tears.

"Get out of here? With the law? You're finally following in your big brother's footsteps?" Chet laughed so loudly that the librarian turned and shushed us.

"You're my baby brother," I whispered, "not my big brother. And it's not following you but stepping in the shit that you leave behind. The police think I'm involved in a murder."

"Who? That comic that was killed?" Chet asked, wide-eyed and chuckling.

"You know about that?"

"Hey, just because I'm on the streets doesn't mean I'm illiterate. I read the papers. Are you involved?" he asked. I could tell he'd be thrilled if I said yes.

"Of course not. Did you know Bob Patterson?"

There was a long pause before he answered, "I'm a bum, Mannie, not a killer."

"There's this detective that seems to be zeroing in on me..."

"Brott?"

"Yes," I said, surprised that he immediately knew who I was talking about.

"That explains everything," Chet said, acting proud that he knew something I didn't.

"You know Brott?" I asked, afraid to listen for the answer. If he knew him then this thing was bigger and more complicated than I thought possible.

"I hate that sonofabitch," Chet said. If we hadn't been in a library I think he would have spat on the ground in disgust.

"Does he hate you?" I asked.

"Big time."

"Why?"

"He's convinced I killed his sister."

I could swear that the world stopped moving on its axis. It was hours before it started rotating again.

"And did you?"

"In a way, yes."

"One of the first things you learn as a comedian, is that sometimes being funny is just not appropriate." Mannie Grand, guest lecturer, Humor 101, Minneapolis Technical College.

14

"Do you remember when I was the bartender at Vinkle's?" Chet asked.

"How could I forget? It was the only legit job you ever had," I replied. Vinkle's was St. Paul's most notorious hangout for derelicts and crooks. Hardly a week went by that it didn't make headline news.

"Brott's sister was a topless dancer at Vinkle's," Chet informed me, his voice softening at her memory. "Her name was Cinnamon."

"Nice name. Was it her real one?"

"Yeah, I think so. Cinnamon Brott ain't a name you'd give yourself," Chet snorted, and then added quietly, "She was a real nice woman. She had just turned thirty when I met her. It was kinda sad. She was doing more than just dancin' for bucks, if you know what I mean."

"She was a hooker?" I asked, wondering only briefly how two siblings, John and Cinnamon, could be so different. Then I remembered that the slimy guy sitting across the table from me emerged from the same gene pool that I did.

"Vinkle was her old man — and I mean old man — the guy had to be at least 65. He was also her pimp. If anyone gave him two hundred bucks, he'd give 'em Cinnamon."

"Two hundred sounds like a lot," I told him, thinking of the low-rent crowd that must have hung out at the bar.

"She would have been worth it," he told me, drifting off for a moment. I had never known Chet to be attracted to any woman. It was ironic that it was the sister of a man that I found attractive.

"Cinnamon had a great body but it was her face that would make your heart stop," he continued. "She had skin—it was like white dishes or something—there wasn't a flaw on it. Her hair was dark red. Her eyes were green. They sparkled. 'Like a Christmas tree,' she used to say. She'd laugh while she asked me if I wanted to check out the presents underneath. She was something all right, but she was off limits to me. She belonged to Vinkle."

You could have fought for her, I thought to myself. You could have gotten both you and her out of there.

"Where was her brother?"

"He was a rookie cop by then and still living at the foster home that Cinnamon had run away from. Cinnamon told me they weren't close like brothers and sisters should be. I told her that was something I could understand."

Feeling a pang of guilt, I was surprised that Chet thought we could ever be close. The thought of bonding with Chet made me shudder. One of us would have to change to have that happen, and I didn't want it to be me.

"Sounds like you and Cinnamon were friends," I told him.

"Yeah, we were. Though Vinkle was always hanging around. In between dances she'd sit at the bar and we'd talk. She was always pounding down whiskey and talkin' about what shitty karma she and her brother had."

"How?"

"Their parents were killed in a car accident. Her dad was drunk when it happened. She and her brother drifted from one foster home to another. When she was thirteen, she and Brott were placed in a home of religious fanatics."

"Define fanatics."

"They went to church every Sunday."

"Get out of here!" I said, sarcastically. "Every Sunday? No way!"

"Cinnamon ran away when she was sixteen," Chet continued. "Brott stayed behind. He was three years younger than she was."

The same age difference as Chet and me.

"That had to be tough on Brott."

"She said he wanted to stay."

"How did she die, Chet?"

I watched Chet's face change, in a matter of seconds, from a tired, old cynic's to a hurt young man's. Chet was twenty-six again. He breathed a slow, deep sigh before he began.

"She did have one fault," he told me as his eyes filled with tears. "She was a drinker. Big time. Some nights she'd pack away a fifth of Wild Turkey."

"Did she ever get treatment?"

"No. You think Vinkle wanted her normal? I told her she should get some help. I even looked up AA for her in the phone book."

"She never went?"

"Nah, she just talked about going. She even talked about going that last night."

Chet stopped for a moment and looked around to make sure no one was listening before he continued. "It was thirty below that evening. It was a nasty winter. We'd already had fifty inches of snow and it was only January.

Cinnamon had been hitting the bottle pretty hard. By the end of her shift, she could barely stand up, much less dance. Vinkle had left earlier to meet his buddies at the bar down the street. Cinnamon was supposed to join him.

At closing time there were a couple of cops hanging around outside the front door. In her condition, they woulda tossed her in detox. She hated being in detox. Her brother usually showed up to lecture her and give her a Bible to read.

Cinnamon asked me if she could stay at the bar for a while, but I knew that Vinkle would get suspicious if we hung around after closing, if you know what I mean."

"I know what you mean," I told him. I waited until Chet looked like he could talk again. "Go on."

"I told her she had to leave. I wrapped her in her coat and buttoned it for her. I even helped her put on her cap and mittens before I pushed her out the back door."

"Had she acted like that before?" I asked, watching Chet brush away a tear with his calloused grimy hand.

"A dozen times. Once, she was locked out, she pounded on the door to be let in. And like always, I just turned up the jukebox and kept mopping. When the knocking stopped, I figured she'd left."

"But that's not what happened, is it?" I asked.

"No. This time it was different. She blacked out," he continued. "I was the one that found her the next morning. She was frozen, sitting up in the alley. She looked like an ice sculpture."

"I don't remember you getting in trouble for any of this," I said to him.

"I didn't. The coroner said it was an accident. Besides, nobody seemed to care. To them, she was just another drunk."

"Does her brother think it was an accident?"

"No, he thinks I should have been charged with manslaughter. He thinks I should have let her stay in the bar."

So do I, I thought to myself.

When I saw Chet's face, I knew, no matter what he told himself, he felt the same.

"I'm in an aerobics class for large ladies. We meet in the basement of my church. Of course, we were on the first floor when we started last week." Mannie Grand, Masonic Home for Seniors.

15

Sometimes I feel awed by the absurdity of life, particularly my own. After nearly a decade of carefully planned avoidance, I had confronted my criminal, yet sane, brother in a public library. I found myself mourning for Cinnamon, a woman I previously hadn't known existed. And in the midst of my emotional turmoil, I was scheduled for an audition, hoping against all odds to grab a two-minute television spot on Comedy Central.

But at least I finally understood why Brott was focusing on me. He assumed I was like my brother. My job now would be to convince him that I was as unlike my brother as he was unlike his sister, Cinnamon.

I wondered if there was a chance I reminded Brott of her. According to Chet's description, Cinnamon and I looked nothing alike, but we were both performers. Cinnamon danced on table tops to make everything all right in her world, while I bartered jokes for acceptance in mine.

Brott and I could be friends, I decided. We had a lot in common. We'd spent a lifetime trying to make up for the sins of our ancestors.

It wasn't going to be easy to make Brott understand that I was nothing like my brother, but then nothing in my life was easy. Even the audition I was going to would, more than likely, turn out to be a waste of time.

I had promised my personal manager I'd show up for the tryout. And besides, virtually every Twin Cities comic would be there. I wanted to listen to every word that was uttered. I wasn't expecting someone to say "I killed Bob," but someone might say or do something that would lead me to the killer.

I climbed the four flights of stairs to my manager's office. Ray Raymond is a legend in our industry. During the sixties, he lived in New York City where virtually every young comic genius walked through his agency's door, including Steve Martin and Whoopi Goldberg. Ray told each of them they would never make it. He told them to keep their day jobs. He suggested Whoopi learn hair dressing.

He was convinced that only his select few—Martha Louise and Roger Addison—would make it. They were the ones he truly believed in. I hope they kept their jobs because they never made a dollar in show business. Yet, he believed in them, and it proved once again that if Ray liked you, you were destined for nothingness.

Ray liked me a lot.

"Where the heck have you been?" Ray yelled as I entered the reception area of his cluttered office suite.

"I had a meeting," I answered, as I surveyed the packed room filled with hopeful faces. This was too big a lottery for anyone to ignore.

"It's not every day I hold a major television audition," Ray snarled.

No, I thought, it's once in a lifetime.

No one could believe that the Comedy Central reps chose Ray's office to hold auditions for new talent. Maybe they found his obnoxious behavior and ludicrous appearance intriguing. They might have thought his cigar chomping, plaid pants, and porkpie hat were planned retro, rather than just bad taste.

Ray's life was a tribute to the fifties, the decade of his golden youth. The one good year of his life, 1955, was the year the Brooklyn Dodgers won the series and the year that Ray got laid for the first and probably last time.

Looking around I saw that LaVonne, The Kid, Milos The Magnificent, Lenny, and even Grant Cuddler, not to mention a dozen or so other comics that I knew and about forty others that I did not. When Comedy Central's in town, every Twin Cities actor claims to be the world's greatest stand-up.

"Does anybody know what they're looking for?" LaVonne asked. She had dressed in her punk look, chains and a leather motorcycle jacket. She's always careful not to be taken for a dumb blond. "Beige with an attitude" is what she calls herself.

"I'm sure it's not me, unless they're casting for Ernest Borgnine's love toy." I said as I slid out of my coat.

At forty-one I already knew that the ship called "fame and fortune" had sailed by me. But I honestly couldn't think of anything else that I could possibly do to earn a living other than stand-up.

Every Sunday, wherever I happened to be, I would sit down with the classifieds and read the job listings. One by one I would cross them off. The bottom line was, I didn't care about my bottom line. My needs were few and comedy covered them all. When I am sixty-seven and still entertaining in nursing homes on Saturday afternoons, I may want to reconsider, but for now, I plan to stick with comedy.

"It would be incredible to be picked," Milos The Magnificent said as he pulled a five-foot scarf from his front pocket and tied it in a massive knot. He uttered a quick "pouf" and voila! — the scarf was in an even larger knot than when he started. Embarrassed, he began working furiously to untangle his failed trick.

"It certainly would," I smiled at him, wondering how someone so uncoordinated was attracted to magic. But then, the unfunny are often drawn to comedy, just like dieters are pulled toward Sara Lee.

I picked up the magazine *Amusement Business* and started to page through it. I glanced up from the article I was reading and looked at Lenny. My stomach knotted. How could he manage to show up for an audition, yet couldn't attend the funeral yesterday?

"Maybe I do have a chance after all," I said, putting down the magazine and pointing proudly to my oversized hips. "Are we talking Comedy Channel here or what?"

"I think the food channel is more like it," LaVonne piped in.

"I'll take it," I said. "Any TV is good TV."

"Hey, Lenny," I said, trying to sound confused rather than anxious, "I thought you were working at The Funny Bone in Indianapolis this week?"

Lenny's already ruddy face darkened. His wildly bushy eyebrows almost met in the middle, which looked like a raccoon's tail was glued above his eyes.

"I canceled," he said, not looking at me.

"Why weren't you at the funeral then?" I asked.

"I was halfway across Wisconsin by then. I got as far as Milwaukee when I called the club to bow out," Lenny answered, his body rigid with tension. I could see his jaw tighten. I couldn't tell if he was dealing with grief or guilt.

"Why didn't you call me? I could have worked The Bone for you," The Kid yelled as his undeveloped chest tried to puff out in anger.

"Come on, Kid," I reprimanded, realizing how inappropriate it was to have even the slightest confrontation at an audition. "Lenny's had a hard enough week without you badgering him."

"But it was The Bone!" The Kid stormed off to the other side of the room. He was one step away from throwing a temper tantrum.

"If they were casting for Home *Alone 4* he'd have a damn good chance," LaVonne said, making light of his youth and immature behavior.

"Why doesn't he act his age?" Grant asked.

"He is," I smiled, my buried maternal instinct rising to the occasion. I looked at The Kid. Sometimes he was eighteen going on eight, but with the amount of talent he possessed, he could act whatever age he wanted to.

"Do the police have any leads yet?" LaVonne asked Lenny as she bent over and tightened the shoelaces on her leather high-heeled boots.

"How should I know? The damn cops haven't told me anything. I can't even go home. My apartment is still blocked off by yellow crime scene ribbons."

I noticed that small beads of sweat were collecting on Lenny's furrowed brow. If he was the killer, he'd last one minute under interrogation.

"Where are you staying?" I asked.

"Milos is letting me sleep on his couch," he said, not sounding grateful. I looked at Milos. Not a flicker of reaction crossed his face.

The two of them were up to something, but I had no idea what.

Ray Raymond leaned out of the audition room, his chartreuse-green and lemon-yellow porkpie hat angled jauntily on his balding head. He yelled, "The Kid!"

"Break a leg," I told my young friend.

"Kill," Lenny encouraged The Kid.

"Make them scream!" Milos mumbled.

All of our lingo is violent. Humor is very often a verbal assault.

I watched The Kid put on his "I Am Somebody" strut and glide across the room. Each of us desperately wanted him to be chosen and each of us just as desperately wanted him to lose.

The problem with show business is that there's not enough stardust to go around. Each of us is both a comrade and an enemy.

"Have you done a TV audition before?" I asked Milos.

"Lots of times," Milos answered.

I've always been uncomfortable around Milos. He mumbles rather than talks. I still can't tell if it's shyness or arrogance. Or perhaps its his ominous look that frighten me.

His long black hair is pulled into a ponytail at the nape of his neck. He's six foot one of muscles and looks like he could break a tree in two as easily as a toothpick. With his dark clothing, long hair, silver jewelry, and tattoos of skulls and roses, he looks like a vampire direct from Central Casting.

He claims to have been featured all along the West Coast, yet I wouldn't hire him as an opener. Still, he looks successful. And in this business, that alone will often get you the job.

Milos is one of the many comics who hoodwink their way into a club and a career. The comics are usually booked one club at a time, and never work the same room twice. They roam from comedy club to comedy club.

He may have a string of clubs and burnt bridges behind him. Maybe that's the reason he moved here and, more importantly, perhaps that's why he always appears to be hiding something.

"Did you always live in Seattle, Milos?" I asked him,

wondering why I'd never heard of him before he came to Minneapolis. Seattle's produced some of the best loved acts in the business. A Seattle comic can work every day of the year without once having to go east of the Rockies.

"I've lived all over," he responded, barely audible. "I'm always moving."

"Do you know Howie Lind or Rick Polstad?" I asked. Both are good friends of mine and Seattle comics.

"Sure, but I doubt if they'd remember me. I was doing open stages when I met them. They were already headliners."

"I thought you middled out there," Lenny reminded him. Even Lenny didn't trust what Milos The Magnificent said about his career. He always said Milos was full of bullshit. That's one of the reasons I was surprised he was staying at his apartment.

"I never worked an A Room in Seattle," Milos finally answered tersely. "I did mostly crappy one-nighters across Washington and Canada. That's why I left."

"Are there any one-nighters that aren't crappy?" LaVonne asked.

"Nope," we answered in unison.

"Didn't you have a home club?" I asked, using the phrase we comedians use for the local club where we developed our acts.

"Sure. The Laugh Pit," he answered, looking at me carefully as if he was trying to figure out what I was after. "It's closed now."

I wanted to continue grilling him when the office door opened and The Kid came out of the back room, smiling. He was happy with his audition.

"Great," I responded straight from my heart, and then sighed an inward "Damn," straight from my ego.

"Mannie Grand," the L.A. rep called in that condescending 'I know if I'd ask you to, you'd kiss my butt for the rest of my lifetime' voice.

I stood up and walked toward the audition room. My clan started yelling their own twisted version of support.

"Go for it, Granny!" LaVonne shouted, as the rest of them slung similar ageist insults.

I turned, looked at my dearest friends and then, smiling,

waved at them — using only my middle finger. I turned around and mimed using a walker as I toddled into the audition room. I could hear the gang laughing behind me.

That has always been one of my problems. I've always wanted to make the comedians laugh more than the audience. I'm destined to be a comic's comic.

The dark-headed bimbette inside the audition room asked me "And you are?"

"Mannie Grand," I told her proudly, wishing I had made a more commanding entrance than that of a nursing home resident.

"And you've been doing comedy for...?"

"Eighteen years," I tried to say proudly, but my shame overrode any pride I was feeling. The Hollywood generation in front of me knew that if comics don't make it in the first thirty seconds of their career, they never do.

"God, that's almost as old as I am," the baldheaded, pimply faced, ear, nose, lip and eyebrow-pierced teenage/Hollywood producer giggled.

My constant supporter, Ray, knew my self-esteem and confidence were melting like the Wicked Witch of the West. He didn't help by adding, "You guys are gonna love her. She's not as young as the rest of 'em but she's just as funny."

Why didn't Ray just take out a 45 and finish me off? They shoot old comics, don't they?

Charley's Deli & Submarine Shop was located a few blocks from Ray's office and I headed there after my audition. My feet dragged almost as much as my spirit.

I caught a glimpse of myself in a store window. I looked like Lou Costello in drag. Maybe what I needed was a partner like Bud Abbott was to Lou. It seemed evident I wasn't going anywhere on my own.

I had accidentally stepped on the baldheaded, pimply faced, ear, nose, lip and eyebrow-pierced teenage/Hollywood producer's foot and, while begging for forgiveness, spilled coffee on Ray's cream shag carpet. I stuttered and stammered my way through a bit I have done perfectly a thousand times before. The L.A. children were kind to me, though, pretending to have tape in the camera when I performed.

I figured the food at Charley's couldn't make me feel any worse. And I wanted to see how Charley was dealing with Bob's death and the frenzied media attention that followed it.

Charley was a friend to most of the show folk in town. He was the only one who would run tabs for struggling artists. As long as he thought they were trying, Charley would let entertainers charge ten meals before they were cut off. Then he'd usually give them the meals for free.

Charley's Deli was closed for three days following the murder. According to the newspapers, the police shut it down to search for traces of cyanide.

The extensive news coverage had to have hurt Charley's already ailing establishment. Charley had come to America from Greece and had worked for forty years, managing to build, as he liked to say, "nothing from nothing." He once told me he worked fifty hours a week and the pay-off was minimum wage.

I considered Charley a good friend. He always asked me how my career was going and I'd lie and say great. Then I'd ask him how the deli was doing and he'd grin and say wonderful. We carried on with our polite deceptions from there. Carrying on usually involved a limited discussion on the wonders of Greek philosophy. Charley glowed when he spoke of the glory days of Athens when the Greeks ruled the civilized world. I always bit my comic's tongue and never reminded him it happened two thousand years ago.

"How 'ya doing?" I asked him as I opened the door.

Charley was sitting behind the cash register, the ever-present paperback in his hand.

Books are another bond we share. They also may be the reason that neither one of us is financially solvent. We both love the pleasure of getting lost in words and rarely look up at the costly world around us.

"What are you reading?" I asked as I sat down at the counter.

"The Burglar Who Traded Ted Williams," he smiled, knowing that I am Lawrence Block's biggest fan.

"That's a good one," I told him.

"They all are, Beautiful Lady."

Charley always called me beautiful. It's hardly a term that fits but, as Charley likes to point out, to a Greek man, all women are Aphrodite.

"I haven't seen you for a while," he said.

"You could have seen me at Bob's funeral," I said, not wanting to be mean but needing to know why Charley hadn't come.

"Ah, the funeral," he sighed. "I couldn't handle it, Mannie. I couldn't see Bob lying there dead, knowing that I had something to do with it."

"It's not your fault someone tampered with your food," I told him.

I watched Charley as he stood up slowly and started to rinse vegetables. Charley's work station is directly behind the counter. I tease him that he looks like a Kabuki chef as he chops away at lettuce and tomatoes.

"Has the publicity hurt your business?" I asked, noting that it was lunch time and Charley and I were the only ones in the place.

"How can I tell?" Charley replied honestly. "My business is never that great. But then, it's not so bad. I make enough money to pay my rent and buy my books."

"Not a bad life," I reminded him.

"Lunch is on the house today," he said with a shy grin.

I learned long ago that it was useless to argue with Charley when he wanted to feed you.

"Thank you," I answered.

"How about some pea soup? It's got those little croutons on the top."

"Sounds good."

"You're a little sad today?" Charley asked as he placed a large bowl of steaming, thick green soup in front of me.

"I just bombed at an audition."

"Are you sure?"

86

"Look out your window. There's a mushroom cloud hovering over the city."

"There's always tomorrow," he said as he reached behind him and grabbed a chocolate donut he then placed next to my bowl.

Like any good Greek man, Charley had found the way to this woman's heart.

"Have the cops been here today?" I asked.

"Sometimes twice a day the police are here. Mannie, I'm a suspect? Me, Charley Demopolous!"

"Are you sure?"

"There is this one detective. His name is like a hot dog. You know, Brott? He always asks the same questions over and over but it's like he doesn't hear what I say."

"What does he ask you?"

"About that night. He asks me how I made the sandwich. He asks if there was anyone in my deli when I made it. He asks why I closed the shop early. I showed him how I made the sandwich, step by step. I showed him how I wrapped it up and how I put it in a bag and walked it over to The Box. I tell him it was in my arms the entire time. The next day he comes back, and asks me the same questions all over again."

The phone rang and Charley walked over and picked up the receiver. At first he spoke quietly in Greek but then he began to yell. I didn't understand the language but he was clearly upset. When he hung up the phone, he grabbed a paper napkin and wiped his damp forehead.

He paused before he turned to me and said, "That was my landlord. He's always worried about getting his money. *Malaca!* I have never once missed a payment in 20 years."

I wondered how many Greek landlords there could be in a city built by Norwegians and Swedes.

"What were we talking about?" Charley asked, still frazzled by the phone call.

An upsetting thought entered my mind and I forced it to disappear. I refused to listen to that tiny but vocal part of my brain that said maybe I didn't know Charley as well as I thought I did. I refused to see anything but goodness in Charley. He

87

deserved at least that much from me.

"You were telling me about the sandwich," I said to him patiently.

"That night, I wanted a little fresh air so I walked to The Box."

"And you didn't set the sandwich down along the way? Or give it to anyone to hold?" I asked.

"Of course not. I'm not senile yet, Mannie."

"And no one came up to you?" I asked, knowing that even though Charley wasn't senile, if he did have a fault, it was that he trusted everyone.

"Who's interested in a sixty-some-year-old man carrying a two-foot sandwich?" Charley laughed, amused at his own image.

"Was there anyone unusual on the streets that night?"

"Mannie, I walked down Hennepin Avenue. What do you think? In the first block alone, I saw three women with no eyebrows and one who had Medusa's hairdo."

"What was going on at the club when you arrived?"

"Dave was busy at the door, collecting the cover charge. He had paid me ahead of time for the sandwich."

"Does he usually do that?" I knew that Dave hedged on any bill he had to pay, especially one that was not yet due.

"Never, but Dave stopped by the day before. He had just come from picking up a comedian at the airport."

"Was it Grant Cuddler?" I asked, wondering why Grant had arrived a full day before he needed to.

Charley nodded, saying "That's when I met him. Dave said he was a big shot. He said he had been on The Tonight Show."

"Did Dave say anything else?"

"He asked Grant if he wanted anything to eat but Grant said he wasn't hungry."

"So, Grant knew you were making the food for opening night?" I asked, my mind reeling with possibilities.

"Yes."

"Did Grant talk to you at all?"

"Not a word," Charley answered.

"The next day, when you arrived at the club, what did you do?"

"I went straight to the dressing room and put the sandwiches on the table. No one was in the room so I left."

"Nothing unusual was going on?"

"No."

"Did you talk with Dave?"

"No," Charley answered with total sincerity.

My gut clenched. I remembered Lenny's story about Dave yelling at Charley for being late. LaVonne, too, had heard it.

"Dave didn't say a word?" I asked cautiously, not wanting to embarrass Charley. "He didn't yell at you for being late?"

Charley looked confused and then started chuckling. "Oh that? Dave always yells at me for being late, even when I'm early. He does it so much, I don't even hear it anymore."

"So everything seemed normal?" I asked.

"Yeah, like I told the police, everything was the same, except for the Santa Claus guy."

"You saw Santa Claus?"

"Only his shadow. You know how the club's marquee is so bright that it lights up part of the alley?"

"Yeah."

"When I walked past the alley, I saw someone running. It was only the shadow of a bearded fat man. But he was carrying a pack on his back, you know, like Saint Dick."

"That's Saint Nick. Did you see his face?" I asked. A sickening feeling came over me when I realized what my next question would be.

"Like I said, only his shadow," he answered.

"There's no way you could tell me if he had a knife scar across his face?"

"I couldn't tell," he said.

I uttered a silent prayer: "Please God, don't let it be Chet."

"I'm domestically challenged. Just yesterday my roommate asked me if we could, at least, keep some ice in the house. Yeah, like I've really got the recipe for that!" Mannie Grand, on-stage Kewadin Casino, Upper Peninsula of Michigan.

16

I was sitting on my closet floor, tossing taped-together shoe boxes to LaVonne. She caught the boxes in mid-air and threw them on the bed. There were at least five dozen shoe boxes piled high on the chenille spread.

I'm a packrat. I have almost every piece of paper that has drifted my way since grade school. Somewhere in the mess were the receipts from a road trip I went on with Bob.

I grabbed the last box and crawled out of the closet. LaVonne was happily going through the debris. She appreciated any chance to tease me.

She giggled as she held up a piece of yellowed paper. "Why do you have a 1973 K-Mart receipt for a $3.97 blouse? Why do you keep this crap?"

"Taxes," I answered flatly, aware that asking LaVonne to help gave her permission to have fun at my expense.

"You don't earn enough money to worry about taxes. Let's toss everything," she said brightly, forgetting my anxiety about discarding anything.

"No," I said through gritted teeth. I knew she would never understand the rationale behind my irrational behavior. "Keep focused on what we're looking for."

"Look!" LaVonne said, picking up a pink card with a small yellow tassel hanging from it. "Your high-school prom dance ticket? Caribbean Nights was the theme? How corny."

"Hey, seven hundred plastic coconuts hanging from the rafters—you'd never have guessed it was a gymnasium in Minnesota."

"What color was your dress?"

"Kind of a burnt blue," I answered.

"I've heard of burnt orange but never burnt..."

"I was a smoker then. Chiffon and Marlboros don't mix."

I continued opening boxes, wishing I wasn't so organizationally impaired. Though the boxes had labels like "Comedy," "School Reports," "Family," it meant nothing. I always crammed papers into the nearest box, no matter what the label claimed, thinking I would remember where everything was when I needed to. I never did.

"Hey, look at this!" I said, amazed at the trivialness of the junk I managed to accumulate. "This is a receipt from the first crappy motel I stayed at on the road. The mattress was wrapped in heavy plastic. Every time I rolled over a loud crunching sound woke me up."

"Are you sure you saved the receipt you're looking for?"

"I save everything," I answered, as I glanced at my ninth grade essay, *Jacques Cousteau, Hero of the Deep.*

I knew the receipt I was looking for was in one of the boxes. I remembered the trip well. Bob and I were booked at Monkey Business, sixty miles southwest of downtown Chicago.

I laughed and joked the whole way, telling Bob that making the audience laugh would be as much fun as giving candy to a baby. I didn't tell him the baby was psychotic.

Chicago audiences treat comedy the same way they react to a sporting event. If our jokes didn't score, they'd let us know the hard way. Instead of heckling, they threw popcorn, peanuts, and beer bottles.

"I found it," LaVonne yelled, holding up the Visa receipt. The hotel record was stapled to it.

Bob and I were both out of cash that week and we charged everything on my card. Bob had promised to pay me back at the end of the week when the club paid us.

I looked at the hotel receipt. We didn't charge breakfasts because our hotel provided a continental breakfast. (I've often wondered which continent depends on day-old donuts and watered-down Tang to jump-start their day.) The only meals we charged were our lunches. We ate dinner at the club. The only other charges were for long-distance phone calls. The telephone calls were the reason I remembered the trip.

I had no idea how many long distance phone calls he was making. They were all billed to his room which was backed by my credit card. If I had known what he was up to, I would have taken away his calling privileges.

I've often been on the road with comics who charge everything to my credit card when they're out of cash but I've been stiffed only twice. (In fact, one famous comedienne—dark hair, pudgy—still owes me $2.38 for a box of tampons.)

But this was more than a few bucks. At the end of the week, the hotel phone bill came to $225 and Bob was only earning $250 for the week.

"Who the hell were you calling?" I asked him after we checked out of the hotel.

"Friends," he answered. "I didn't think you'd mind. You said I could make a few calls."

"A few calls? I only wish I had stock in Ma Bell. What if you died or ran away? I'd be stuck with the bill."

"I'm not the type to run away," he laughed, handing me the $225 in cash. "And when I die, I'll leave you a little something."

"You sure did, Bob," I thought as I saw that every call on the bill had the same area code. Who did Bob know in Seattle?

"The great thing about being a road comic is that you get to meet all kinds of people. The bad thing about being a road comic is that you get to meet all kinds of people." Mannie Grand, speaking at Richfield High School's Career Day.

17

I've always liked Seattle. Nestled between the Olympic Mountains and the volcanic Cascades, its warm inviting air reminds me of pine-scented bath salts. And, of course, I can easily get there by Amtrak.

My fear of flying is second only to my fear of mountain driving. I, therefore, not only endure but relish the thirty-seven-hour train ride from St. Paul. It's worth all the jiggles and bumps just knowing that I'll be rewarded by the sight of trolleys, snow-capped peaks and my many anticipated binges at the outrageously wonderful Pike Street Market. As soon as I pack my bags, my mouth starts watering.

Seattle overflows with the good and the glorious. It's corny, but it's as pretty as a picture postcard. I just make sure I never turn the card over and look at the other side.

Seattle is schizophrenic, like a drug-head from the sixties who struggles to be a member of polite society. There are two Seattles—one of hiking trails, bike pathways and outdoor concerts of be-bop jazz. The other, darker, Seattle is a quick ticket to hell.

The city's underbelly feeds on heroin, festering on the angry remnants of grunge rock. In Seattle, when kids decide to put a band together, they don't just name the group. They christen it by shooting up.

In greater Seattle, there are an estimated 14,000 needle-loving losers. It's legal to buy needles over drug store counters. And, if the heroin user finds it too inconvenient to stop by Walgreens, there's always the Free Needle Exchange booth.

I met my first junkie in Seattle. I was introduced to her by the comedy club's emcee. After my opening night, the emcee invited me to hear his favorite alternative band, Decaying Grandmothers, at a grunge bar down the street.

I normally avoid rock clubs after I perform. I've already received enough second-hand smoke to last a lifetime. But my first night in Seattle I wanted to celebrate working the West Coast. I was up for anything, or so I thought.

As we neared the bar, not only could I hear the music blaring from half a block away, I also thought the club was on fire. Smoke was seeping through the doors and windows. It took a few minutes before I realized the smoke was from cigarettes.

The house band that was playing was another Nirvana rip-off. Each band member had long, greasy hair, worn jeans and a plaid flannel shirt. I remember thinking I must be getting old because all I kept repeating was "Hey, didn't we do this during the Vietnam War?" (Why is it the bad stuff keeps coming back? Like bell bottoms and Jerry Lewis? But not the good stuff, like panty girdles?)

We edged our way through the crowd until we reached the farthest corner of the club. We sat at a table with seven kids who were barely out of their teens. They were completely stoned.

At first, I didn't recognize that it was a heroin-induced high. I thought they were stoned on grass, but then I realized that even the strongest weed couldn't produce what I was witnessing.

The emcee's girlfriend barely acknowledged my presence. Her lips sort of smiled when I was introduced and then she drifted away, trapped in her own bliss. I sat at that table for three hours. The entire time, the emcee kept looking at his girlfriend and saying over and over, "Isn't she great? Isn't she beautiful?"

She wasn't even moving. She could have passed for dead. If his sexual preferences continued to evolve, his next sexual obsession would be necrophilia.

For the rest of the week, whenever the emcee asked me if I wanted to party, I turned him down. Six months later the club owner called and asked if I'd come back. I told him only if I could bring my own emcee.

As soon as the Seattle club owner called me I had called Bob and asked him to go with me, but he refused. When I asked why, he said he'd been to Seattle once and vowed never to return. Besides, he told me, he found out one thing while he was in Seattle: He wasn't funny there.

Now I wondered what else Bob had discovered in Seattle.

"I guess I'm finally getting a celebrity status. I actually have my first stalker. Well, it's a man from a collection agency."
Mannie Grand at The Chicago Improv.

18

I hadn't told anyone about the favor Bob had asked me the day he died. I wasn't being paranoid, just cautious. So far, the media had blown everything out of proportion. If they discovered I drove to Duluth to pick up Bob's bag of marijuana, they'd be like piranha in a blood bath. If they found out what was really in the bag, I might as well start knitting a noose.

At three p.m., on the day he was killed, Bob had showed up unexpectedly at my apartment door. LaVonne had just left to use her two-dollars-off coupon at Great Clips. I was perfectly content sitting in my overstuffed armchair, munching on Ho Hos and reading The *Burglar Who Studied Spinoza* when the doorbell rang.

I threw on a green chenille robe over my tartan plaid pajamas and rushed to the door. When I opened it, I was surprised to see that it was Bob. He never dropped by without calling first. From the look on his face, I knew something was wrong.

"Come in," I said, licking chocolate crumbs and marshmallow goo from my fingers.

"Am I interrupting anything?" Bob asked, looking frazzled.

I noticed how worn his gray wool overcoat was looking and that two buttons were missing. The torn front pocket had been repaired with green thread. His muffler was frayed and his gloves were coming apart at the seams. His boots were torn and repaired with duct tape.

"No, I was just reading," I answered, wiping the sticky chocolate off my chin. I held my book behind my back, trying to conceal the fact that I was using a Butterfinger wrapper as a bookmark.

"I'm so glad you're home," he said, taking off his coat.

"You want some coffee?" I asked, wondering if he and Lenny had fought or if he had lost a good gig, the two most likely reasons for his appearance.

"Sounds good," he said, following me into the kitchen.

Bob sat at the table while I made a pot of Jamaican Jitters. He started playing with the salt and pepper shakers, juggling them in the air until he failed to catch the salt and it crashed to the floor, breaking apart as it hit the tiles.

"God, I'm sorry," he said, reaching for the broom to wipe up the mess.

"Just leave it, Bob," I told him. "I'll get it later. Why are you so nervous? Is it because you're working The Box this week?"

I knew that working with a headliner as infamous as Grant could turn anyone's stomach into a food processor.

"The Box?" he asked, looking even more confused.

"You know, working with Grant Cuddler."

"Oh, yeah, sure," he said absent-mindedly.

The foggy, anxious wreck in front of me was hardly the sweet, calm, unassuming guy I knew.

"What's wrong, Bob?" I asked.

"Nothing, really. A little problem."

"You didn't come here just for coffee," I reminded him.

"You're right," he said sighing. "I'm probably being paranoid, but I've got a problem that could turn into a major disaster for me. Do you think I'm being paranoid? Maybe I should just go home..."

Bob stood up hesitantly, then looked around dazed, and sat back down again.

"Just tell me the problem and let's see if I can help," I said to him, feeling exasperated.

"God, Mannie, will you help? I don't know who else to turn to."

"You've got to tell me what the problem is before I can agree," I said. If it had anything to do with lending money, he was out of luck.

"I drove to Duluth last night," he said.

"Were you performing at the Brew & Bowl?" I asked. Every

Monday night the bowling alley has a comedy show in their banquet room. Duluth is an international port, located on Lake Superior, that connects to the St. Lawrence Seaway. The comedy night attracted Minnesotans, Canadians, and international sailors. Comics never know if the audience spoke English, French or Kurdish.

The room is small but it pays extremely well, twice as much as any other club in Minnesota. We figured the higher-than-normal pay was because the drive to Duluth in winter was a long and treacherous one. It hadn't surprised anyone that Tom Dilbert's car had crashed.

The city was built on steep hills with winding streets. The lake-effect of the wind tossed snow around as if it were trapped inside a glass snow dome. Beautiful as the town is, going to Duluth in January is one of my least favorite things to do.

"I drove there to do a guest set," Bob said. "Canadian comics were working the room."

"Did you stay at the condo?"

"No. I stayed at a hole-in-the-wall on the edge of town. The Twin Pines Motel."

"That place looks really run-down."

"It's worse than that. But then, what can you expect for $18.95 a night?"

"Filthy shag carpeting, cheap paneling, moldy showers," I answered.

"And more. This particular dump had a religious theme," Bob said.

"How so?" I asked.

"The motel's lobby had a giant velvet painting of Jesus on the cross. The owner wore a sweatshirt with a lamb painted on it and the words "He Loves Ewe.""

"Sounds like a safe place to stay," I told him, preferring that environment to the hooker or biker motifs I've endured. "At least Christians won't rip you off in the middle of the night."

"No, they were God-fearing, good people and that's my problem."

"Explain."

Bob got up and started to pace back and forth across the

kitchen floor, kicking the spilled salt out of his way.

"Mannie, you know me, don't you? You know I'm not a drug addict."

I didn't even bother to respond. I just laughed at what I thought, at that time, was a ludicrous question.

"I don't even take aspirin," Bob continued. "But once in a while, I smoke a little marijuana."

"How much?" I asked, not surprised. A lot of folks do a joint here or there. But I also know that when a person insists they drink or smoke "only a little," I multiply their answer by seven.

"Maybe a total of ten joints a year."

I did the multiplication in my head and came up with the real answer of a joint and a half a week.

"That doesn't sound like much," I told him, relieved it wasn't more.

"It isn't. I've never even bought a whole ounce before last night."

"You scored grass in Duluth? Who in the world did you buy from?"

"The headliner from Winnipeg. He almost got caught carrying it across the border. He wanted to get rid of it before he went back home so he gave it to me for next to nothing. Thirty bucks."

"If you're so worried about having a whole bag, just flush it away," I told him, a little pissed that he'd bothered me with his anxieties. I had enough of my own to deal with.

"I can't," he said quietly.

"Why not?" I asked.

"I left it in Duluth," Bob answered, his face as white as a white-walled tire.

"At the motel?" I asked, knowing that if the answer was yes, Bob was in trouble.

"Yes."

"Jesus, Bob, how could you do that? Were you stoned?" I asked, amazed at his stupidity.

He nodded. "I only had one joint but it must have really hit me hard. When I left this morning, I forgot to put my duffel bag in the car. I only realized it when I drove across the Minneapolis city limits."

"Do you think the motel owners will call the police?"

"I'm positive they have no idea what's in the bag. The duffel has a lock on it."

"So what's the problem?"

"When I called the motel manager, he told me I had to pick the bag up today or he'd mail it. That's his policy. No exceptions. Buying a lid of grass is only a misdemeanor but receiving it through the mail is a Federal offense. We're talking decades in prison."

"Then just turn your ass around, go back and pick up the dope," I almost spit the words at Bob. I was furious. I knew what he was going to ask me to do.

"I have to perform at The Box tonight," he whined. "Even if I left right now, there's no way I would be back for the eight o'clock show. You know how slow I drive."

"Get someone to take your place."

"Dave will fire me if I do that."

"Dammit, Bob. I don't want to drive all the way to Duluth to pick up your grass," I screamed at him.

I looked outside the kitchen window. Snow had started to fall and the wind had picked up. I envisioned my wrecker of a car and doubted that the tires could survive another three hundred miles for a trip that should not have to be made.

"Mannie, please," Bob begged me. "You don't know what it's like to be afraid of going to jail."

"Yes, I do," I told him. I've feared prison and anyplace else I couldn't escape from all of my life. I knew the agony he was going through. "You owe me, Bob. You owe me big for this one."

"I know I do," he responded, smiling for the first time since he came in.

So I drove to Duluth that afternoon. I spent the whole time cursing my own wimpiness and arguing out loud with an incendiary conservative AM radio show host.

My heater wasn't working so I wore three layers of clothing. I felt and looked like a giant toddler who could barely move in her snowsuit. A large piece of cardboard was tied to the grill of my car to keep the engine heat from escaping, forcing it to re-circulate inside of my car. We cold and poor in Minnesota always have a few survival tricks up our well-insulated sleeves.

The road was slippery but driveable. The three-hour one-way trip turned into five. Finally I saw the lights of the motel. Never once did it cross my mind that the police might have been waiting for someone to pick up the duffel bag. I trusted the motel owners, remembering my years as a Baptist.

The place was as tacky as Bob had described. Orange and green were the dominant colors, with dashes of yellow and red for contrast. Over the cash register were handwritten signs stating "Married Couples Only" and "We don't lend money." In the center of the lobby was the massive velvet painting of Jesus. It could have been tackier. I once actually saw a velvet painting that included not only Jesus and Elvis but also five dogs playing poker.

I rang the bell and a young woman came out of the back room looking as if she stepped out of an episode of "Little House on the Prairie." Her waist-length hair was pulled back by a simple ribbon. Her cotton print dress hung loosely on her, nearly touching the floor. She wore no make-up or jewelry. She didn't look at me when I spoke to her.

"I'm here to pick up a bag that was left in Room 9 last night," I told her.

She reached under the counter, handed me the bag, turned and left. She said nothing to me. She didn't ask for ID. She didn't ask me to sign anything. She just assumed I was as honest as she was.

I took the bag, got into my car and drove off. Ten blocks later I pulled over to the side of the road, shaking so badly that I couldn't drive. It had finally dawned on me that the Duluth SWAT team could have been waiting for me in the lobby. I never felt as stupid in my life as I did at that moment. Until, that is, days later, when I finally got around to opening the bag.

I had hidden the locked bag under my bed as soon as I got home and hadn't touched it in the days since Bob's death. Finally, I decided it would be wise to flush away the marijuana. Had I gone through with tossing the contents in the toilet, the Tidy Bowl guy would be cruising around in a yacht.

Inside of the bag was a change of underwear, one smelly T-shirt, no grass, and one million dollars.

I had been setup after all, but not by the motel owners or the cops. I had been setup by my good friend, Bob.

I remembered Bob's beleaguered, poor-soul image sitting at my kitchen table. I remembered him shopping for clothes at the Salvation Army. I remembered him waiting in line to accept Federal commodities, gratefully receiving five pounds of old cheese and boxes of broken crackers.

Looking at the million dollars, it occurred to me that all the time I thought he was poor, he was really a rich eccentric. Then I thought maybe he was a wacko who washed aluminum foil and counted sheets of toilet paper while stashing away a fortune in a mattress. Nothing made sense.

Before I opened the duffel, I couldn't come up with one reason why Bob was killed. Suddenly I saw a million reasons to knock him off.

I picked up the bills and held them lovingly in my hands. I'd never had more than a few hundred dollars in cash at one time. There I was, caressing $100 bills that were spread out on my $19.95 cream-colored bedspread from WalMart.

The greenness was dazzling.

"The funny thing about a Geo Metro is that it comes with a vanity mirror — if you had any vanity, you wouldn't be driving a Geo Metro." Mannie Grand at UpChuck's Comedy Club, St. Charles, Illinois.

19

I counted the money twice. Each stack was held together by a paper strip that was imprinted with "$10,000" in red ink. I put every stack back in the bag, except for one. I slid the bag under my bed and put the ten grand I had lifted into my cosmetic bag.

Until then, the only money in my possession was the $84.51 in my wallet. There were two reasons I needed more than that. One was to help solve Bob's murder and the second, if necessary, was to escape.

I was slipping the cosmetic bag into my purse when I heard LaVonne yelling for me to run to the living room.

"Get in here!" she screamed. "There's breaking news on Bob's murder."

I ran out of my bedroom and down the hallway. For days, WXLZ had been suggesting that the police were close to an arrest.

I reached the front room just in time to see Charley's precious and terrified face appear on our 19-inch screen.

"Oh, my God, not Charley!" I yelled, falling onto the sofa.

"Shh-h," LaVonne said, tears already flowing down her face.

The screen dissolved into a tape of Charley's arrest, an hour earlier. The Minneapolis SWAT team had descended on his tiny deli. The video of the arrest showed a dozen camouflaged attack men capturing one frightened senior citizen holding on to what appeared to be a dangerous plastic spatula. Charley was still wearing his white apron and Twins baseball cap. His wrists were handcuffed behind him. My heart ached when the policeman placed his hand on the top of Charley's head and forced him into the waiting squad car.

Charley's mug shot appeared on the screen. He looked confused. There was a front shot and then a profile shot that showed the nobility of his Athenian nose.

"Oh, Charley, " I sighed, wondering if life could possibly become any more insane.

The announcer came back on the air stating that "Murderer Charles Demopolous was arrested today in connection with the killing of comedian Bob Patterson." Then he covered his butt by adding "I mean, alleged Murderer."

"Oh, so adding alleged at the end makes up for calling him a murderer on prime-time television?" LaVonne hissed.

"Did you see how Charley was shaking? He'll never make it to trial."

We watched as the announcer continued destroying any chance for fairness.

"Demopolous," the anchor enunciated slowly, "is the owner of Charley's Deli, located on Marquette Avenue in downtown Minneapolis. An anonymous hotline tipster revealed that although Charley has resided in America for over forty years, he immigrated illegally to this country."

"Shit," I mumbled. On top of everything else, Charley didn't need the immigration department on his back.

"Do you think he'll be deported?" LaVonne asked.

"I have no idea," I said, shaking my head in disbelief.

The announcer continued with his assault. "An informed source, close to WXLZ, also verified that Demopolous is heavily in debt."

"Who isn't?" I yelled at the screen, tossing a throw pillow at it.

I tried not to listen as the announcer ended with, "The debt is rumored to be a large gambling debt. Sources at Mystic Lake have verified that he was a familiar face at the casino. Lori, over to you."

Lori, the roving reported, stood in front of The Comedy Box where Dave Olson and a few comics were waiting. They were all smiling. For most of them it would be their first TV credit.

"As you know," Lori, the roving slut, began, "Bob Patterson was killed at this very site only one week ago by cyanide hidden in a sandwich prepared at Charley's Deli. It is ironic that The Comedy Box, which is dedicated to making people laugh"—the camera zoomed in and Dave waved—"is home to such tragedy."

"I can't believe that jerk Dave is waving," LaVonne said, tossing another pillow at the screen.

"Standing next to me is the club's owner, Dave Olson," Lori continued, her already faux deep voice deepening even more. "Mr. Olson, we've noticed that you've managed to keep your club open all week in spite of the tragic occurrences."

"Yes," Dave said with a practiced pause. "I truly believe Bob would have wanted it that way."

"Your wallet wants it that way, you sniveling piece of shit," LaVonne screamed.

"Are you surprised at Charley's arrest?" the reporter asked Dave.

"Yes, I am. Charley's always seemed a decent sort. But then, you never really know someone else, do you?"

"Why don't you just pull the switch on the electric chair, you munchkin bastard!" LaVonne doesn't swear often but when she does, it's a joy.

"I can't take this anymore," she announced and clicked off the TV.

"This makes no sense," I told her, feeling like everything in my universe was turned upside down. "It's not even logical to think Charley would kill Bob."

"No, but then who ever said killing is logical," LaVonne said.

"Are you implying that Charley is a psycho?" I responded in anger, disregarding the fact that LaVonne, too, must have been feeling overwhelmed. "I've eaten at least two hundred times at the Deli, so why didn't he do me in? Or anyone else that ate there? Charley is quiet, shy, and...."

"Just the kind of guy that ends up being the killer, at least in the movies." LaVonne sighed. Composing herself, she said, "I'm sure he didn't do it, but did you know he had a gambling problem?"

"He doesn't have a gambling problem, LaVonne. Charley plays bingo. If bingo was a crime then they'd have to arrest every Catholic in this state. They have no proof he killed Bob."

"Well," LaVonne said hesitantly, "none except for the fact that Charley's sandwich had a cyanide garnish."

"Details, details," I said, dismissing her point. "There's not one single reason why Charley would do it."

I turned around and stomped noisily back to my room where a million reasons waited for me.

"Flight attendants are always giving me those tiny liquor bottles as souvenirs. I'm not a drinker, but I found the bottles come in really handy for trick-or-treaters at Halloween." Mannie at The Giggle Factory and Outlet Mall, Marshfield, Wisconsin.

20

An annoying, slow violin version of "You Ain't Nothing But a Hound Dog" assaulted my ears the next morning. Amtrak reservationists had put me on hold. I was so irritated that I hung up before I could cancel my reservation to Missouri.

Ironically, even though Charley had been arrested, it was more important than ever that I stay in town. I had to find Bob's real killer. My good friend Charley was being held on Murder One at the Hennepin County Detention Center. As far as I knew, Charley had no family to fight for him and none of his friends could put up the $500,000 bail.

And it looked like, as far as the police and media were concerned, Charley was guilty until proven innocent.

If I had to, I would stay in town and work as a temp to survive while I continued my investigation. I was determined to get Charley out of jail.

I had always thought I'd be a good cop. It was time to see if I was right.

I had gotten up at four a.m. When the alarm sounded, I turned it off immediately. Our walls are paper thin and I didn't want to wake LaVonne. She still didn't know about the money I had hidden in my room. I needed to get it out of the apartment.

I needed to get rid of the money until I decided what to do with it. It was a distraction. There were too many other things I needed to care about, like Charley or my investigation.

If I lost the dough in the process of hiding it, then I lost it. I didn't ask for it in the first place. And besides, if there was such a thing as blood money, this was it. The only thing I knew for sure was that it was no longer safe to keep it in the apartment.

107

I put the duffel bag full of loot into a black trash bag and tied the top with red and green paper ribbons —the kind that can be curled with a scissor's edge. And because at times my sense of humor becomes twisted, I did just that.

The streetlights were still on and dawn was hours away as I slid down the icy sidewalk to my car. I drove until I reached the hiding place I had in mind. It took over twenty minutes to successfully hide the money. I knew that sometimes the most public place can be, in a city that rushes by, the most private.

It was five-thirty before I reached home again. I had stopped by Einstein's Bagels and bought a half dozen. I made a pot of coffee and opened the Star Tribune and Pioneer Press in front of me. I cut out the articles concerning Bob's murder and Charley's arrest and taped them carefully into my notebook.

According to the *Pioneer Press*, an anonymous caller suggested the police check the landfill in Shakopee, a small suburb south of the Twin Cities. The police searched for two days until the deli's trash bags were located. Inside one of the bags were discarded deli menus, rotting garbage, and a broken industrial-sized jar of mayonnaise. It was the same brand used at the deli. Inside the jar was enough cyanide to kill every comedian in town.

The article didn't mention whether there were fingerprints on the jar. The trash containers behind Charley's Deli were accessible to thousands of pedestrians who walked by daily. Unlike major cities such as New York or Chicago, we don't put garbage under lock and key. The jar could easily have been planted in his dumpster. I've seen the same size mayonnaise jars for sale at Sam's Club. Not for one minute, while I was reading the stories, did I allow myself to believe the picture that was being painted of Charley.

I forced myself to dismiss the nagging memory of the last time I had visited Charley, the day that he became so angry on the phone. Until that morning, I didn't even know that Charley had a temper.

What was it that Dave Olson had said in the newscast — that "we never really know anyone." I shivered, shocked that I was giving credence to anything that Dave said. I was beginning to realize how little I knew of myself, much less anyone else. For one thing, I never thought I would be capable of keeping money that didn't belong to me. Now I knew how much easier it would be to keep the million bucks than to give it up.

Of course, I knew that if I kept it, I could never take the chance of depositing it in a bank. Yet even without a penny of interest, it could serve me well for the rest of my life. If I continued to earn the meager income that I did from comedy, and spent only $20,000 a year from the stash, I would be ninety-one years old before it ran out and I'd have to start working again. Meanwhile, life, with money, would be so much easier.

Amazingly, even with an extra twenty grand a year, I would not change that much. I wasn't interested in a flamboyant lifestyle. I just wanted one that bordered on middle class. I wouldn't buy a flashy car, just decent tires for the one I have. I would buy four at once, not just one at a time. I would also abandon my duct-taped muffler, get the heater repaired, and fix my antenna so I'd never have to listen to talk radio again.

Life would be good.

I would buy new clothes. I would get my hair cut at a real salon rather than the beauty school where I grit my teeth when the nervous student, holding newly sharpened scissors, approaches. I would get a new computer, one that has more memory than my watch, and link onto the Internet. I would dot com myself all over the world. I would get new headshots, this time from a highly paid professional photographer, not the guy at Sears Photo Studio. I would allow the photographer to airbrush as much as he wanted. My new photos wouldn't even look like me.

Life would be very good.

I would not waste the money. I deserved the money. I would be a steward with the money. And Bob, most of all, would be happy that I, of all people, had it. Didn't he say he would leave me a little something when he died?

I would have kept the money and done all of that except for a recurring vision of one frail philosopher and cook, sitting alone on a worn cot, surrounded by madness. I never knew that money (never having had any substantial amount of my own for a reference point) would allow me to so completely believe in my own bullshit. I almost convinced myself to keep the dough.

But I wouldn't. I would find out where it came from and more than likely, return it. Hopefully, in the process, I would discover who killed Bob and free Charley.

I cut another article from the *Tribune*. It focused on The Comedy Box. In all this media hype, it looked like Dave had convinced the paper to do an article on the club's history. In it, he spoke of his own illustrious past. He bragged about the many comics he had sent on to stardom. He spoke of his own humble beginnings.

The newspaper article mentioned everything about Dave except the fact that he had spent five years in Stillwater State Prison.

I had already tried to find out from the comedians who hung out at The Box about Dave's prison time. No one would say a word. They were afraid that if Dave found out, they would never work his club again. They were right. Like most tyrannical kings, Dave demanded complete loyalty.

And he got it, except from the few who had lost the stars in their eyes—like Licker—so-called because he licked his lips at the end of every sentence he spoke. Licker had walked away from comedy a dozen years ago. Like most B-room comics, and unlike myself, once he hit forty he came to his senses and opted for benefits and a weekly paycheck.

Rumors had him working downtown at an insurance agency. With enough phone calls and using his real name, Jeff Anders, I finally located him in the IDS tower.

When I walked through his office door, it was obvious that Licker had used his talent and charm to full advantage in the business world. The agency bore his name. Licker saw me through the window of his office when I entered and rushed out to greet me.

Comics like each other better once they're no longer comics. When Licker was doing stand-up, he barely acknowledged my existence. He considered me a newcomer not worthy of his time.

"Mannie Grand," he smiled and rushed toward me, a grin on his wrinkled but still-freckled face. His arms surrounded me and

I felt like I was being hugged by a bear. His natural exuberance made him a good salesman. It would be difficult to deny Licker anything.

"Mannie Grand," he repeated, licking his lips.

We walked into his office. His walls were covered with numerous plaques and awards. He was a member of the Chamber of Commerce, The Rotary Club, and The Lions. His desk was covered with family photos. A color 8x10 featured him with his arm around St. Paul's archbishop. Licker was a citizen of distinction. No one could tell from being in his office that at one time Licker did the best fart jokes in the business.

He and I began to reminisce about the good old days for him and the not-so-good old days for me. He told me that he never went to comedy clubs anymore, but always read the entertainment listings. He said he smiled whenever he saw my name and wondered why I never made it big.

He asked me if I was still doing my bit on personal ads. I said yes and so was everyone else. We laughed at that. We both understood that not only has every joke been written, but it's also been stolen.

I finally got around to asking him about Dave Olson. Whenever I speak to former comics, and Dave's name comes up, the reaction is always the same. It was no different with Licker.

Licker told me that Dave was one of the reasons he quit comedy. He was tired of fighting with him for bookings and decent pay. He refused to continue working for squat while Dave dressed in Armani suits and vacationed in Boca Raton. When he did quit, he took full knowledge of Dave's past with him.

"It's a sign of what a sleazy business entertainment is when Dave Olson is considered a respected businessman," Licker began, as he sipped his coffee. "Let me tell you what's really behind Dave."

"Go for it," I said as I reached over and grabbed a jelly bean from a dish on Licker's desk. The dish was in the shape of a demolished pink and silver '57 Chevy.

"Do you know about X World?" Licker asked.

"Wasn't that the club Dave owned before he turned it into The Box?"

"He didn't own it. At that time, he was only the manager. The word on the street was that the club was owned by a Chicago crime family."

"What was it like?" I asked, reaching for another bean.

"Your basic sex club," he said with a faint smile that told me he approved of such places.

"Strippers and such?" I asked.

"Nude dancers, porno movies for a quarter and hookers available upon request. The joint was dirty. I don't mean that in a sexual way though it was that. It was just a filthy little dive that brought in a lot of money. It catered mainly to frat boys from the U and conventioneers from Iowa. The strippers were all low-rent whores. One of them had to be fifty years old."

"You hung out there?" I asked, glancing at his award from the mayor for distinguished citizenship.

"I was only doing research for my act," Licker laughed, his tongue nearly touching his nose. "Hey, I was 18 years old then. My brain ran on testosterone at that age. Seeing a naked lady, even a fifty-year old one, was high on my priority list. X World was lax on checking IDs. The fake one I used said I was a thirty-one year-old-Asian."

Licker lost his train of thought for a moment with a jaded memory or two before he went on. "I used to go there with a couple of other comics like Jimmy Foltz, Mickie, and even Bob Patterson every now and then."

"Bob?" I asked, surprised.

"Every male in his twenties who lived in Minneapolis eventually showed up at X World. I mean, who could resist their slogan—Boobs and Beer for a Buck."

"Animals always appreciate alliteration," added I.

"I was actually only there a half dozen times before it shut down, but I remember Dave," Licker continued. "At the time, I was very impressed with him. I mean, here he was, only a little older than me, and he held the best job in the world. Free booze and undressed women — it didn't get any better than that."

I smiled at Licker. I had always admired his honesty. Thank God, in many ways, he was still the same.

"Tell me more," I said.

"Dave was nicer back then. I could tell he'd never read a book in his life, but he was fun. He always had a joke and a smile on his face."

"Get out of here! Dave, happy?"

"Yeah, amazing isn't it? He knew every punch line there was. You couldn't walk up to him without him saying, 'Did'ja hear the one about...?' In fact, I always thought it was ironic that I turned out to be the professional comedian and he didn't. He used to talk about becoming the next Milton Berle."

"In the 18 years I've known him, I don't think he's ever once mentioned that he wanted to do stand-up."

Licker paused before he sadly added, "Prison changed him."

"It must have. The Dave I know doesn't have a funny bone in his body. What was he in for?"

"Manslaughter."

"Wow," I mumbled, understanding why Dave sometimes looked as if he had the weight of the world on his shoulders. He did.

"I can't imagine what it was like for him to be in jail," Licker continued, "but I do know that prison can change a person forever. I see it in this business all the time. A nice enough guy does right by his family, and then one day, when his mind drifts off for a second, he turns a corner and runs over an old lady. Within days he's charged with manslaughter. Mannie, that's why it's so important to have proper insurance coverage. Have you thought about..."

"Can we just talk about Dave?" I asked, reaching over to grab another jelly bean and then stopping myself. I didn't want to feel indebted to an insurance salesman.

"Sorry," Licker laughed, "it's easy to fall into my sales rap, but I believe in insurance. Maybe that's why I'm so successful. In a split-second, a life can be changed forever."

Yes, it can, I thought to myself, remembering poor old Charley.

"There's a couple of versions of what happened that night," Licker continued. "There's the one that Dave confessed to and the jury bought. Then there's the one that Dave told me when he was a little too high on tequila one night. I personally believe the latter version."

"Tell me," I said, my investigator instincts tingling at Licker's words. I knew I was finally getting close to some answers.

"It began at two a.m. on a Sunday morning," Licker said, staring out the window. "X World was closed for the evening and Dave was in the back room, working on the books. The owner was arriving that afternoon from Chicago.

"It was the semi-annual meeting with the big guy. Dave was only twenty-one at the time, but he possessed an innate sense of business. X World was more profitable than ever. Dave was beginning to learn how much crime did pay.

"The owner wasn't due in until the afternoon. Dave was getting ready to leave when he heard the front door open. He reached over and grabbed a pistol that he kept in his desk drawer. The owner, unexpectedly, had arrived early."

"Dave accidentally shot the owner?" I asked.

"No, as soon as he saw who it was, Dave set the gun down. The owner liked to show up unannounced, just in case a manager was erasing the ledgers at the time. He also arrived with two associates, both weighing over 300 pounds, just like their boss did."

"Birds of a feather," I stated.

"Exactly. I guess the boss liked to have men around that were as big as he was, in case he needed to 'persuade' anyone. But Dave didn't need any persuasion at that point. The books were fine. Everything was as legit as it could be.

The boss, 'Hugs' was his nickname, was pleased."

"I'm afraid to ask why he was called Hugs."

"You have a good reason to be afraid. Supposedly he had hugged one of his cronies a little too long."

"And his pal died?" I asked, already knowing the answer.

"You got it. Anyway, Hugs told Dave that he was now part of the family and he'd always be taken care of. The two sat and drank together. Hugs was tossing down countless shots of tequila as Dave reveled in his own good fortune.

"When Hugs asked Dave if there was anything he could do for him, Dave shook his head and told Hugs he had everything he needed. He told him about his favorite stripper and the special tricks she provided in private. He also told Hugs about his brand new ebony and ivory sports car.

"Hugs, who was nearing sixty and probably bored with large breasts and bouncing bottoms, perked up at the mention of Dave's car. Hugs announced that he'd never driven a Corvette.

"Dave didn't let anybody drive his car but how could he say no to Hugs? Hugs was intoxicated by then to the point where his speech slurred and his vision was impaired. Dave looked at the henchmen for a clue as to what to do. Their faces registered no response at all.

"Dave found himself putting the car keys in his boss' hand and telling him to take the car for a spin."

"Bad idea," I said to Licker.

"You got that right," Licker agreed. "It was only an hour later that Dave heard the club's front door open and turned to see the two goons carry in Hugs. He was unconscious and bleeding all over.

"The henchmen had followed behind their boss as he swerved north on I-35 at eighty miles an hour. When their boss took the exit for Highway 96, they did too. The exit was only 35 or so miles from downtown Minneapolis, but back then, the area was remote and rural.

"Hugs was just past the exit when he hit a teenage boy running along the side of the isolated road. The boy was only fourteen years old. He was so excited about his first high school track meet that he was jogging on the country road at 5:00 a.m. The boy was thrown in the air like a rag doll hit by a train.

"The henchmen pried Hugs out of the Corvette. They didn't even bother to check on the boy. They could tell he was dead as he sailed past them. All they were interested in was getting their boss and themselves the hell out of there. The henchmen left an empty tequila bottle on the floor of the car, though they smashed it into tiny pieces so that fingerprints were not readable. They left only enough remnants to prove that the driver had been drinking.

"They piled Hugs' enormous carcass into the limousine. They drove him back to the club to wait for the family's physician to fly in from Chicago on a private jet. The frightened doctor operated

115

on Hugs on the club's chipped mahogany bar top.

"Hugs survived. The boy didn't. By that afternoon, when the police arrived at Dave's apartment, it was Dave who admitted to driving the hit and run. It was Dave who was sent to prison, not Hugs. And it was the young and happy Dave that died the same night that the boy did.

"X World," Licker continued, "was shut down until Dave was released from prison. On the day that Dave was set free, the club was sold to Dave for the grand sum of one dollar—unless you add the cost of five years of Dave's life."

"Some story," I said, wondering how differently Dave's life would have turned out if Hugs hadn't killed the boy. Would Dave be a comic now instead of a club owner? A friend instead of an enemy?

Licker continued. "And that's how Dave became the owner of The Comedy Box. The funny thing is, right before you called this morning I was sitting here thinking about Dave and all the crazy things that went on there." Licker handed me a couple of colorful insurance agency brochures.

"Did Bob's murder trigger your memory?" I asked.

"No, it wasn't that. I was looking at the entertainment section, you know, reading the comedy listing of who's where, and I noticed an ad for the club in downtown St. Paul."

"Bomber's?"

"Yeah, that's the joint. Their ad featured photos of the upcoming acts. I had no idea that one of the bouncers at X World had become a comic."

"Who?"

"Gee," he said hitting his forehead, "what does he call himself now? Something really corny."

"Chuck Giggles? Mark Mirth?" I asked, my brain clicking through every hack comic in the Twin Cities.

"Not those. Wait a minute. I remember..."

"Who," I asked impatiently, watching Licker's tongue do its exercise.

"Milos The Magnificent."

"My brother had one of the first cell phones in the world. Then he got a TV for his prison cell, a microwave, a computer....." Mannie Grand, at home, working on a new bit for her act.

2 1

On my way to the Hennepin County jail I stopped at a Middle-Eastern deli and purchased two gyros and a pint of taramusalada — a wondrous pink Greek spread that is made from fish roe. Besides the mysteries of Rex Stout and Ruth Rendell, a good taramusalada was another passion that Charley and I shared.

I didn't know if I would be allowed to bring Charley food or anything else. It was amazing, given my ancestral heritage, that I didn't understand the proper etiquette for visiting day at the Big House. It should have been second nature to me. The Grands always considered a trip to the slammer a family reunion.

Sitting in the waiting room were twenty or so other visitors hoping to see their loved ones. Some looked as freaked as I did; most looked a bit bored.

My prison phobia was gaining momentum and I hoped it would not overcome my desire to comfort my friend. Not only did I need to see Charley, I felt quite certain that he needed to see me.

I breathed deeply and started to repeat to myself what I knew about the case so far. Over and over, like a mantra, I stated the facts, hoping that sudden insight would fill in the gaps.

"Bob was murdered with cyanide while performing at The Comedy Box. The poison was found on the sandwich from Charley's shop. LaVonne and Grant Cuddler were also on the bill that night. Bob's roommate, Lenny, was also at the club and backstage prior to the poisoning.

"Sixteen hours before the murder, another comedian, touring Seattle performer Tom Dilbert, had been killed in a car accident in Duluth. This was the same Dilbert who had forgotten his luggage at the condo. Bob had agreed to deliver it to Duluth. I assumed that, once in Duluth, Bob opened the luggage and found a fortune in cash. In a panic, Bob left the bag on purpose at the motel. In the scenario I was putting together, Bob asked me to pick up the bag for him and, like a fool, I did. Bob was killed. I hid the money in a very public place. Charley was arrested on suspicion of Bob's murder."

I realized that Bob's recent refusal to go with me to Seattle might or might not have something to do with his murder. Milos The Magnificent is from Seattle.

First I thought it must be drug money. Then counterfeiting crossed my mind. And, of course, gambling. Always gambling.

I decided Grant Cuddler might be a problem gambler. When he and LaVonne and I ate at Denny's, I recognized the fire in his eyes when he spoke of gambling. I had seen that same burning rage in my own.

And if he was a compulsive, a million dollars would be a drop in that bottomless bucket. To a compulsive gambler, no amount of money was ever enough. Whatever they won, they gave back. I should know.

And of course there was Dave Olson, his prison record and his connection to organized crime to consider.

I repeated my ruminations for the fourth time when the door opened and a female jailer came into the room. Her hair was the color of a fire hydrant. She was built like one, too. She looked like Lucille Ball on steroids. She quickly scanned every person in the room and walked directly over to me.

"You're Mannie Grand?" she asked as she traced my body with a portable metal detector.

I nodded my head.

"Isn't that a man's name?" she mumbled.

"Actually Grand can fit anyone," I told her, tired of the same old questions about my masculine moniker.

"Your real first name," she grunted, as she bent over and traced my Nikes with the electronic device.

"Mannie stands for Amanda," I answered.

"Amanda fits you better," she told me and, for a change, I

did not bother to argue. She opened my purse and rummaged through it, removing my make-up case and a rat-tail comb. She looked inside my make-up bag. There was only Maybelline. I had had the foresight to leave the money in my glove box. She also removed my pens and nail file.

"You can't bring any of this stuff with you. What's in the paper bag? Food? You can't bring food in. You could'a put something in the food."

Like cyanide? I wanted to ask.

She looked inside the bag and took a deep whiff as the aroma of hot gyros and freshly steamed pita escaped.

"Do you want me to throw this out for you?" she asked, already palpitating with desire.

"Sure," I answered.

"Follow me," she told me and turned and walked out of the room. I grabbed my almost empty purse and followed her down a long corridor. She opened a door to an office and with her finger, pointed for me to go into it.

"Wait in here," she said, as she quickly shuffled away with Charley's and my lunch in her hand.

It took two seconds before I realized that I was in Brott's office. The shelves on the walls were filled with baseball and hockey trophies from Brott's high school and college days. There was a graduation photo of him with what I assumed were his foster parents. I did not see a photo of anyone who could be his sister Cinnamon.

"Take a seat," Brott said, coming into his office. An unlit cigarette dangled from his lips. The building, like other official buildings in Minnesota, was a smoke-free environment. But Brott was the kind of man who always wanted to make a point, however insignificant.

Once again, I noticed that he was not wearing a wedding ring. I also noticed again that, for a man in his late forties, he was in great shape. The sleeve of his dark blue shirt was so tight against his over-sized bicep that I couldn't have slipped a fingernail beneath it if I wanted to.

And I did.

Brott was a paradox, with his perfect weightlifter body and

dangling, carcinogenic cigarette. He was someone who wanted to be at the top of his game and at the same time was toying with something that assured he would never get there. I'm always fascinated by kindred spirits who almost make it to the top but fail.

"Mannie," he said, as he sat at his desk and opened a file that was lying on top of his desk. My name, written in large block letters, was printed on the cover.

"Brott," I replied, looking him straight in the eye. I decided to deal with him like I did any heckler who tried to intimidate me. I puffed myself up and acted brave.

"Why are you here?" Brott asked, fully aware what my answer would be.

'To visit a friend," I told him, realizing with a jolt that to Brott, I was as much of a suspect as ever.

"You consider Charley Demopolous a friend of yours?" he asked, the cigarette stuck to his bottom lip. It moved up and down as he spoke, like a cancer-stick puppet.

"Yes," I answered, "a very good friend."

"What do you mean by good?" he asked, leaning back in his chair. He put his massive arms behind his head. The casual pose showed off his expanded chest and flat stomach to their best advantage. He was so very, very attractive and so very much a jerk.

My kind of guy.

"A good friend is the opposite of a bad friend," I responded sarcastically. "But then you probably only have bad ones and don't know what I mean."

"Cut the crap, Mannie," Brott said. "Just tell me about your relationship with Charley."

I looked at Brott and watched his demeanor change in front of me. An ice cold rigidness possessed his body. He turned into metal. He acted as if he were on a mission from God. Part of me wondered if it wasn't a personal vendetta against women, especially female entertainers.

"I met Charley about a dozen years ago," I responded coldly. "His deli is a few blocks from my agent's office."

"Ray Raymond's?"

"Yes," I answered as a familiar quiver raced up my spine. Was there anything he didn't know about me?

"Ray's been my agent for over a decade," I said, and then added, with a comic pause and in my best Groucho Marx voice, "which explains why I'm still working bowling alleys in North Dakota."

Brott showed no reaction. There was no smile or acknowledgment of my little, okay, very little, joke. I realized I had to treat the situation with a bit more seriousness than my usual smart-ass response.

"Okay," I said. "If you really want to know, one day I was walking past his diner and decided to grab lunch. I had never been there before but it looked kinda interesting and cheap.

"When I walked in, Charley was sitting at the counter reading a paperback mystery. No one else was in the place. He looked up and said 'Can I finish this paragraph? I'm right at the end.' I laughed and told him, "Sure." As a reader, I understood.

"I waited a few minutes. Charley closed the book, sighed a sigh of contentment and gave me a meatball sub on the house. Our friendship started that day."

"How often do you see Charley?" Brott asked, his stern face registering no response to anything I said.

"I eat there at least once a week when I'm in town. If I'm on the road, I usually mail him postcards. Once in a while he comes to see one of my performances."

"Have you been to his home?" Brott asked, flipping through the pages of my file.

"Never. I don't even know where he lives," I answered honestly, wondering, for the first time, why I had never asked Charley where he lived. I guess we had more important things to talk about.

"Has he been to yours?" Brott asked, his voice sounding skeptical.

"No." I told him, remembering that when I invited Charley to LaVonne's birthday party he had turned me down.

"Are you involved romantically with him?" Brott finally asked, as if he already knew what the answer would be.

"You've gotta be kidding!" I said, angry that he'd ask such a question.

"Are you sure?" Brott asked.

"Charley's in his sixties, for God's sake!"

"There are women who are attracted to older men," Brott said, a faint smirk crossing his lips.

"Not this woman," I answered, furious that Brott had taken a perfectly innocent friendship and demeaned it. "But if I was going to date an older man, I'd at least make sure he was a rich old man."

"Like Charley?"

"Charley?" I repeated. My mind became one big fog bank. In an instant, I was completely bewildered. Did everyone have a fortune stashed away in a mattress?

"Charley's always broke," I said to Brott. Even I noticed the hesitation in my voice.

"He's not that rich himself," Brott backtracked, and I breathed a sigh of relief.

I had to trust someone in this world and if it had to be a 62-year-old fry cook, then so be it.

"Charley's family has the real dough," Brott added.

"Big deal," I almost spit the words out at Brott. "My dad has one hundred and eleven dollars in his savings account, but that doesn't mean it's mine."

"Have you ever heard of the Demopolo Lines?" Brott smiled.

"The Greek shipping lines? Weren't they the ones that were always competing with the Onassis empire?"

"The Demopolo Lines are owned by the Demopolous family."

"Charley's father?" I said, sinking back into my chair. Everything was becoming more complicated.

"Charley's second cousin."

I took a minute to glare at Brott before I responded, "That's a long way down the family tree. In fact, that's not even the same tree. It's more like a bush sitting next to the tree."

"Not to Greeks," Brott reminded me. "Greek families are traditionally very large and very close. Blood, however distant, is recognized and usually rewarded."

122

I thought of the Charley I knew, a gentle, quiet man. I could not imagine him deserting anyone, much less family. What was he running from?

"Charley's never mentioned anything about his family," I told Brott, wondering what other secrets Charley had not shared.

"Charley was working on the Demopolo Lines when he jumped ship in Duluth. He was thirty-one at the time. He came here illegally."

"Are you going to deport him?"

"I can't. He became a citizen when Congress offered amnesty in '86. Up until then, he was working under the table."

"What a terrible way to survive."

"It must not have been too much of a struggle. The day he became a citizen, he bought the deli with cash."

"Charley doesn't have a mortgage?" I asked, remembering a few days ago at the deli when Charley fought with his landlord on the phone.

"Except for a few bad checks to Mystic Lake Casino, he's free and clear. Did Charley ever talk to you about his gambling?"

"No," I sighed. I had had too many revelations for one day. I didn't want anymore.

I turned my eyes away from Brott and stared out the window. Across the street was City Hall, where marriages either began or ended. The same place birth and death certificates were filed. Everything was a lesson in the yin and yang in life.

If what Brott was saying was true and Charley was a compulsive gambler, I knew why Charley and I had connected. Most addictions are based in a deep sadness. Charley, like me, had damaged roots.

"Can I see him?" I asked, wiping a tear from my eye.

Brott noticed my tears and his voice became quieter, gentler.

"Yes," he answered, "I want you to understand that I'm positive that Charley is Bob's murderer."

"I'm positive he isn't," I lied.

At that moment, I wasn't sure of anyone or anything.

"I'm also sure about something else, " Brott said as he put my file back in his drawer.

"And that is?" I asked him, as I slowly lifted myself up from the chair, my energy totally gone.

"Charley had to have an accomplice," he said, no longer gentle.

I didn't even bother to ask what he meant. I knew he would have uttered, like Bob had, only one word — Mannie.

———————

Twenty minutes later I found myself sitting on one side of a glass wall, staring at Charley, who sat on the other side. For some melodramatic reason of my own, I had envisioned Charley looking like the Ghost of Christmas Past. I imagined him dragging heavy chains as he walked into the waiting room. I was not prepared for the upbeat smiling senior that I saw talking to me through a telephone receiver.

"Mannie, thank you for coming," Charley reached over and touched the glass with his wrinkled hand.

"Charley, you look, I don't know how to say this, well, good..." I told him, reaching over and meeting his glass-barricaded palm. "How do you feel?"

"Okay. They're treating me very well."

"How can you say that? They arrested you and dragged you off in handcuffs." I yelled at him, incredulous at his bouncy manner.

"They were just doing their jobs. Like when I make onion soup, I gotta slice the onions. I don't like to, but I do it."

"We're not talking a daily special here, Charley, we're talking your life."

"Don't worry so much, Mannie. Brott has told me if I'm not guilty they'll let me go. You know, I think he likes you. He talks about you a lot."

"Charley — will you get a grip? He's only interested in me as your accomplice."

"I don't think so. I'm good at this. I often thought I should be a matchmaker. I could do it at the deli. I could introduce customers to each other. Valentine's Day, I could..."

"Do you have a good lawyer?" I interrupted him, wondering if Charley had lost his mind. He should be scared to death.

"Oh, a very good lawyer. He's a public defender. His name is Scott. He's a nice boy. He told me he visited Greece. A little town called..." Charley chatted on before I interrupted him once more.

"Why do you have a public attorney?" I asked. "Brott told me you have money. Lots of it."

"I do?" he asked, looking surprised, as if there was the chance he did have money somewhere that he had laid aside like an old shoe.

"Does Demopolo Shipping Lines ring a bell?" I asked.

"Oh, that," he answered. He acted as if being related to the third richest family in the universe was as common as lint balls on a sweater from WalMart.

"That's my cousin's money, not mine," he said dismissing the importance of my question in the process.

"You never told me you ran away from Greece," I said to him. I needed to let him know that I knew a lot more about him than he thought I did.

"It was more like walk-away from Greece," Charley sighed. "I was, what do you call it, a dark sheep?"

"Black sheep."

"That's it. The real money in the family belonged to distant cousins. I would have to kiss a lot of Greek buttocks to get any of it. I'm not good with kissing anyone's behind, Mannie."

"I've never been a butt kisser myself," I smiled.

How could I have let Brott get to me and make me mistrust this delightful man for even a minute?

"Everything in Greece centered around my cousin Dimitri and his fortune," Charley continued. "When I turned eighteen, Dimitri gave me a job as a cook on one of his freighters. The men on the ship treated me as if I were someone to be afraid of because of my bloodline. Of course, Dimitri was the someone to fear."

"Was he mean?"

"Mean is too nice a word. He didn't get to where he was by saying, 'You first.' The only thing he was interested in was winning, at any cost. He was not a man you'd want to make angry."

"He was vengeful?"

"Like a rabid dog. One day, I just got tired of it all," Charley sighed. "I was sick of pandering to Dimitri, bored with the sea, and wanted a change. I wanted to see America. Like every good Greek boy who spent every Saturday afternoon at the movies, I wanted my life to be like a cowboy movie," he laughed.

"In a way it is," I told him reluctantly, thinking, ironically that most westerns included a lynching or two.

"I'm not a mom but I'm proud to announce that I adopted- - - a highway. I think it's gonna be a great football player 'cause it has such wide shoulders." LaVonne Hastings, eliciting a groan from the audience at her first Open Mike Night, April 1991.

2 2

Monday nights are Open Mike Night at The Box. Open Mike allows amateurs to develop an act and professionals to polish new material.

No one is paid for performing. Professionals are given only eight minutes to perform and the newcomers three. In theory, because no one's being paid, there's no pressure to be funny. In fact, Open Mike Night is the most difficult. It's a place where peers judge and the audience is convinced that because someone's performing for nothing, they are worth nothing.

Monday nights are not a pretty sight. I wouldn't miss them for the world.

Five hours after I left Charley at the jail, I was there with thirty other comedians, and I use the word "comedian" loosely. As soon as someone decides to risk total humiliation by standing on a stage, I respect him or her as a comrade.

The Kid was busy passing out a list of the twenty or so who were selected to perform. Because I was a working comic, I was guaranteed a spot. The newcomers' names were put into a hat and only half were drawn. The newer talent was scattered throughout the line-up, hopefully balanced by the pros who would salvage the show after the amateurs had done everything they could to destroy it.

The line-up for the evening was filled with every stereotypical amateur or pro comic in the world. There was the hyperactive three-year-old boy trapped in a twenty-two-year-old male body. Fresh out of a college fraternity, he was positive that random noises from bodily orifices was the height of humor.

There was the bored and sexually frustrated overweight

suburban housewife who blushed at a PG movie, yet gladly stood on-stage and bantered about the size of her husband's private parts. There was the fifty-five-year-old corporate executive who had been laid off a year before retirement. He was convinced he could turn his pain into profit. There was the newly divorced, newly-permed, newly-implanted babe who claimed she wasn't bitter, yet was blinded not by stage lights but by the tears in her eyes.

I looked at the list and saw that I had been given the number ten spot in the line-up. I went on after someone I had never heard of — a Smiley Jones. I groaned at the name. You only need a goofy name when you're not funny.

On Monday nights I was always more sociable than normal and usually hung around until closing. But I planned on leaving immediately after my performance. I had something more important to do.

The buzz at the club was, of course, about Charley. Most of the comics thought the arrest was ridiculous. One, a notorious racist who believed that white men should rule the world, told me that he was sure Charley did it. I guess Greeks aren't white enough for him.

I noticed that Lenny wasn't there. Unless Lenny was out of town, he was faithful to Monday nights.

The audience was primed for the evening. Because The Box does not serve alcohol on Monday nights, the age limit drops to 18. The 18 year olds, thrilled to be in a comedy club, usually decide the proper response is not applause and laughter but heckles and groans.

Making an open-stage audience laugh is as hard as comedy gets.

I was sitting at the pro table with LaVonne and a few others. I was at the club for more than one reason. I needed to show off. I wanted to let my peers know that, for a change, I was sitting pretty.

I had just bought a round of drinks for the entire table. LaVonne was dressed casually in jeans and a Vikings sweatshirt. Just a regular outfit. For a change, she wasn't imitating a movie star.

I, on the other hand, was dressed to kill in a red cashmere sweater and black leather skirt, both of which I'd found at Value Village Thrift Store. I loved the feel of cashmere but worried that the skirt made my behind look like a dairy herd moving slowly across a field. But the two pieces were the sexiest things I owned and, for a change, I wanted to exude sex appeal.

It was bad enough that I was trying out a new bit about being over forty. Now I would have to go on-stage dressed like an aging tart. The post-pubescent audience could not possibly get it. Last week, at Open Mike, one of the kids yelled "She looks like my mom!"

For the first time in eighteen years, a heckler had left me speechless.

I glanced over the youthful audience. I knew they only laughed at glow-in-the-dark condoms and kegger jokes. I ached with the knowledge that the generation I saw in front of me was the one that would take care of me when I entered a nursing home. I'd probably choke to death when one of their dozen or so earrings fell into my gaping mouth as they spoon-fed me.

The owner of the club, Dave, was back at the sound and light booth. I watched him as he worked the boards. He dimmed the house and turned up the stage lights. He turned on the sound system and played a two-minute tape of rock music.

Remembering what Licker told me, I wondered, for the first time, if Dave longed to be on the stage, not just own it.

Dave clicked on the P.A. system and announced, "Thank you for coming to The Comedy Box. Please remember to keep your laughter to a maximum and your table talk to a minimum. Now, please give a big welcome to your first comic and the host for the evening...The Kid!"

The Kid jumped up on-stage. He danced a funky dance to the fading music and then reminded the crowd that they were "lucky to see comedians before they are famous, and often before they're funny."

His quip got a laugh and it gave him the cue to introduce the first open-stager of the evening — a Jane somebody. This was Jane's first time ever on-stage. He asked us to make her feel at home.

I felt a twinge of excitement. I love watching someone go on-stage for the first time. I'll always remember my first night.

It was at the Old Pickle Barrel. I was the third person up that night. I had what I thought was brilliant material on cops and donuts. I planned to expound on being single and dateless. I envisioned myself gliding through my tightly written act.

Instead, I stammered and stuttered my way through material that, I found out later, had already been used by every hack comic on the planet. I also failed to notice the flashing red light that was my cue to get off stage and I was on twice as long as I was allowed.

But, I was mesmerized by the laughter I heard. Even with all my mistakes, I was killing. I was a star!

Fortunately, I had taped the show that night. Later, when I played the audiocassette back, I had my first epiphany into the powerful delusions that can occur on-stage. I understood why there were so many bad comics. We all possess what comedians call "laughing ears," ears that hear laughter when it isn't there.

The uproarious chuckles I had heard as I pranced about the stage were, in reality, only coughs and occasional sighs. There was not a single, pure laugh during my first six minutes on-stage.

Now, whenever I think I'm doing well, I always remember that first time and wonder if I am being funny or if I'm sporting those ears.

I always hope that a newcomer will, unlike me, kill on their first time up. I want to be lucky enough to see the next comedy superstar when he or she is still "a virgin." But unfortunately, most of the ones I see are like the Jane somebody I was watching.

Jane was wearing a '70s lime-green, polyester pantsuit set off by pink fuzzy slippers. She had scattered green curlers in her hair and draped around her neck was a necklace of red plastic beads the size of golf balls. She was short, a little overweight, and in her mid-thirties, a common age for newcomers. I assumed (correctly it turned out) that she'd just gone through a divorce.

Her voice quivered as she said, "Hello?" and then, "Can you hear me?" The first major groan of the evening arose from the crowd. Her opening line was, "Who says it's easy for a single woman to get laid?" and the material went downhill from there.

LaVonne leaned over to me and said politely, "She's not too bad."

"Not too," I lied, wanting to appear to be supportive of any woman in the business, even when she didn't have a chance in hell. "But she's got to get rid of the costume."

"It's not a costume. She's from Iowa," LaVonne said and we giggled like teenagers.

"Shh-hh," Dave hissed as he walked by. Most of the comics sat in the back of the room. Keeping us quiet and respectful is the hardest part of Dave's job.

I rolled my eyes at LaVonne and watched as Jane squeaked out her bit. It was something about her ex-husband's lack of sexual desire. Her material belonged in a therapist's office, not on a stage.

We politely applauded when she finished. I counted two pity laughs and three groans while she performed. I could tell by her smile that she knew she was a hit.

LaVonne had decided not to perform. She had just arrived from her stint at the Walker and was worn out. Occasionally, she volunteered to help set up exhibits and installation pieces at the art museum.

This past Christmas, she had even gotten me involved. I had found myself, when it was 20 below zero, hanging metal five-foot-high Christmas ornaments across the walkway bridge that spanned Lyndale and Hennepin Avenues. Though Christmas was long gone, the decorations were still there, reminding everyone, as LaVonne put it, to stay in a holiday mood.

As for me, my holiday mood was over. I thought all holiday ornaments should be down the day after New Year's. Glittery things never sit well with us curmudgeons.

LaVonne finished her first stein of Bud Light while I sipped on my second pina colada. I was surprised that being at the club helped me to relax. I needed to be calm and to think clearly. I also needed to become slightly intoxicated—a tool necessary for what I had in mind.

A few other performers came and went as LaVonne and I sat there looking at our watches.

"Can I buy everyone another round?" I asked, burping once in the process. Everyone except LaVonne answered yes.

"You have money to pay for another round of drinks?" she asked incredulously, knowing that the last time I bought anyone a beer was, well, never.

"Yep," I answered as I pulled a c-note out of my pocket.

I waved the hundred dollar bill in the air and motioned for the server, Lila, to come over. LaVonne looked at the bill, then gave me her evil eye.

This was the second hundred dollar bill I had pulled out of my pocket. LaVonne knew those pockets usually contained nothing but mint patty wrappers.

"Lila," I said to the server in a voice loud enough that anyone sitting within 100 feet would hear it. I wanted it known that tonight I was literally throwing money around. I jiggled the bright, crisp bill high in the air.

The Kid walked by and tried to yank the bill out of my hand. We struggled a bit before he finally let go. I wanted every comic in the club see our teasing and, for a change realize that I had more than my fair share.

"Where'd you get so much money?" The Kid asked as he headed, once again, for the stage. "You hooking at the VFW again?"

"Hey, Kid, I'm holding up a hundred dollar bill here," I yelled after him. "Not a five."

Behind me, I heard Lenny's shrill voice. He was apologizing to Dave for being late. I heard him say that he wasn't going to be able to perform as planned. I turned and look at Lenny. He was beet red and sweating profusely. His curly hair was damp from perspiration. If he hadn't been wearing a long wool overcoat, I would have thought he had jogged to the place. Lenny stared straight at me and then turned and walked out of the club.

LaVonne leaned over. "Just where did the money come from? Are you working undercover?"

"Just for myself," I answered. Then she asked me how my investigation was going.

"Not well," I whispered. "I've narrowed the field down a bit but there's always the possibility that I'm wrong."

For example, until Lenny just walked in and out of the club, he was off my list.

"Brott still thinks I'm involved. He thinks Charley and I are the Bonnie and Clyde of the submarine sandwich empire."

LaVonne looked at my hands. "You still have a bit of ink on your fingertips."

After visiting with Charley, right before I left the building, Brott asked me if I would be fingerprinted. I was so shocked by his request that I agreed. One of my major personality flaws is wanting to prove how nice I am. I also wanted to show that I had nothing to hide.

Now I wished I had refused.

Brott led me into a small laboratory where a kind policewoman took my hands in hers and told me lame jokes about a Norwegian couple named Ole and Lena. She rolled my fingers back and forth across the pad like they were little sausages. Chubby digit by chubby digit I left my mark.

Being fingerprinted like a common criminal was one of the many excuses I was using to drink at The Box. I held the little cherry that came with my pina-colada in mid-air. I was dangling it, ready to drop it into my mouth when Dave whispered my name loudly.

Surprised, I dropped the maraschino down my throat and started to gag. LaVonne began pounding me on the back. Two people in front turned around and shushed us.

Dave sniped, "Mannie, when you're through kidding around, there's a homeless person out front who wants to see you."

I finally stopped gagging and looked at LaVonne.

"Chet?" she asked, her eyes wide.

"Who else?" I answered as I stood up, swigging down the rest of my drink in the process. "If I'm not back in ten minutes, tell The Kid you're taking my place."

"Will do," she said. I can always count on LaVonne to cover for me.

I also knew she'd rather come outside and meet my infamous brother but she had enough class not to ask.

She didn't have enough class, however, not to crane her neck around the doorway and peek through the front window.

Chet, looking weary and breathing heavily, was leaning outside against the glass. Ironically, his face rested against my "Appearing Soon" photo.

"How did you know I was here?" I asked, noticing that, once again, my reaction to Chet was always anger. There was no "hello" or "good to see you, bro" coming out of my mouth.

"I'm not an idiot," he said bitterly. "This is where all the comics hang out. You still think you're smarter than me, don't you?"

"I am," I assured him.

"Well, for being so smart, you're pretty damn easy to find. Probably a little too easy for your own good. For one thing, your address is listed in the phone book. When I called your home and you weren't there, I figured you'd be at Amateur Night."

"It's called Open Mike," I said tensely. I had enough problems without adding Chet to them. I knew I shouldn't have gotten him involved.

"Besides, I'm not an amateur," I said defensively.

After all these years, why did this man irritate me so?

"You know, I've been here once before," Chet smirked, looking through the window as he waved to LaVonne. She yanked her head back into the comedy room.

"When?" I asked, swallowing hard as I remembered Charley's description of Santa Claus.

"I've been here a few times. Free passes to this joint are all over town," he said sarcastically, as if The Box was on the same level as the food kitchens that he frequented.

They almost were. The Comedy Box was as easy to get into as a soup line. Dave papers the room, meaning that most of the Box's audience members use free passes to get in. He makes his money on outrageous liquor prices. Four bucks for a bottle of beer that costs Dave fifty cents. However, customers happily choose to believe that by getting in free they're getting something for nothing.

"Did you see me?" I asked.

"I was here when you opened for Lewis Black. I bummed a few more bucks than usual that day, cleaned up at the Y, and came to the show. He was okay. You were better. But I walked out on my tab. I'd never pay that kind of money for booze.

"You were funnier than I thought you'd be. I've always hoped you'd make it big. I know enough about your past to blackmail you forever."

"Yeah? Right!" I said, angry that for a brief second I had started to like him. "Like my past is the sordid one? Like the National Enquirer really cares that Mikey Hagadus gave me a hickey in the seventh grade?"

"That bum made a pass at you?" Chet asked with an amazing amount of self-righteous indignation.

"He was eleven years old," I told him, my anger dissipating into amusement that suddenly, after all these years, Chet was trying to act like a protective brother.

"Why are you here?" I asked, tired of our verbal fistfight, already assuming he was here to get something from me. "Do you need money?"

"I can always use a few bucks," he said, shivering in the cold. He pulled his filthy coat tightly around him.

I hesitated at first, thinking that if I gave him a dollar, I would be starting a habit that would be hard to break. I reached into my pocket and pulled out a ten-dollar bill.

Except for the expense money I took out of Bob's stash, I had only $22.37 of my own money left.

"I can give you a little money now," I told Chet, "but this is it. I'm one step from being homeless myself. Don't come here asking for money again."

"I didn't come to ask for money. You offered it. I came here to tell you somethin'."

"What?" I replied wearily, watching snow fall on Chet's enormous shoulders and wondering how he survived. How could he weigh so much when he didn't know where his next meal was coming from? Did he exist solely on pizza thrown into dumpsters? The forecast called for ten below. Where would he sleep?

I felt my heart opening to Chet and forced myself to close it. I thought every bad thought about him I could. I reminded myself that Chet chose to be on the streets. He chose to be a crook. He'd lied to me a thousand times. He stole from me and

135

everyone else. He was a wanted felon. He looked and smelled like the inside of a garbage can.

He was my three-hundred pound, bouncing baby brother.

"I'm here because of that comic who died," he said.

"Bob?" I asked.

"I've been hearing things. You gotta forget about the murder. The cops already got the guy who did it," Chet said, looking at his feet, watching them make patterns in the snow.

"Charley didn't kill Bob," I said adamantly, though not as adamantly as I would have said it yesterday.

"Charley's an old man. What difference does it make if he fries?"

"Gee, Chet, for a few minutes I started to think that you were human after all. Thanks for reminding me that you're not," I yelled. How did one mother give birth to two so totally different beings?

"Mannie, I'm telling you to quit. Consider this a warning."

"From whom?" I asked, realizing for the first time that maybe Chet wasn't there of his own accord.

"That's none of your business," he answered. "In fact, none of this is your business. It's bigger than you think, Mannie. Besides, there's one thing that humongous brain of yours hasn't thought about."

"What's that?"

"When you finally come face to face with the murderer..."

"Yeah..."

"He's going to be face to face with you."

"Whenever I think I'm in love with a man, I make sure that it isn't because I've been eating chocolate the entire time." Mannie Grand, Holiday Inn Comedy Club, Goshen, Indiana.

2 3

"R—E—S—P—E—C—T...." An hour after my brother's unexpected visit, I was singing along with the cassette as Aretha told it like it is. My eclectic taste ranged from adolescent bubble gum to B.B. King. But tonight, I needed to listen to the Queen of Soul to fight off the depression that was seeping in.

Chet's little visit outside of The Box had upset me. I wanted to believe that he was using Bob's murder to torment me, like the bad old days when he set my doll houses on fire and tried to tie the cat's tail in knots.

I knew someone was behind his visit. But who? Who knew that a "street crazy" was my brother? And if they knew that, what else did they know?

For the first time in his sordid little life, Chet was right.

This was bigger than I thought it was.

I turned the corner. Just as I got to the comedy condo to meet Grant Cuddler *A Natural Woman* began. I had to smile. *A Natural Woman* had always been my favorite make-out song. Too bad I was going to the condo for another reason than that.

Grant had Monday nights off because of Open Mike at the club. When I called to ask if I could drop by, I could tell by his response on the phone that he was convinced we were going to party. Big time.

As I pulled into a parking space, the cassette player started to devour Aretha. It was frustrating but no great loss. I buy all of my tapes at garage sales. The most I've ever paid is twenty-five cents.

I yanked the tape out of the slot. The plastic holder came out easily but the tape stayed in. Two feet of brown ribbon-like film dangled in a hopeless mess. I gave up fixing it and started up the walk to the condo.

The condo is located in Richfield, a southern suburb that borders the Minneapolis/St. Paul Airport. It sits a quarter mile off the primary runway. Dave, of course, got a good deal on the place—a good deal if you don't mind deafening airplane sounds, or the fact that the apartment sporadically rattles.

One visiting LA comic didn't realize how close the condo was to the runway and was in the shower when the first airplane of his stay flew overhead. The entire building vibrated, the soap fell off its holder and a drinking glass in the bathroom crashed to the floor. The comic ran out of the condo, buck naked except for the soap bubbles, screaming "Earthquake!"

A 757 flew overhead as I walked to the building. Both the building and I shook. I looked up and saw that it was the red and white Northwest KLM plane leaving on its midnight trip to London. It left every night at the same time. I was familiar with the nightly departure because it was the only plane I had ever flown on.

Seven years ago, I had agreed to perform at the Comedy Cross at Victoria Station. I forgot I had to fly to get there. I was so terrified that, at the end of the flight, the captain and crew awarded me a "Junior Captain" certificate. The co-pilot had handwritten the words "for surviving in terrifying conditions." The certificate, they told me with a smile, was usually presented to eight-year-olds.

I assumed Grant would be alone. Since LaVonne was his feature act, he didn't have to share the condo with another touring comic. He had the tiny two-bedroom place all to himself.

I walked up the short flight of steps and knocked on his door. I heard a few footsteps and then saw the small glass peephole on the door darken.

"Mannie?" Grant asked, as he peered at me through the hole.

"Yep," I responded.

He opened the door and motioned for me to enter, giving me a half-smile. He quickly bolted the door behind me.

The condo hadn't changed since the last time I was there. It was still sparsely furnished with a dirty tan and gold sofa, two run-down glass-topped end tables and an old pine coffee table covered with magazines, newspapers and overflowing ashtrays. There were also matching looks-just-like-brass, plastic lamps.

On the far wall, seemingly out of place, was a 50-inch, large-screen television, complete with surround sound and picture-in-picture. It featured a full-service cable lineup including HBO, Showtime, and The Playboy Channel. With its mind-numbing extravaganza of entertainment possibilities, Dave managed to fend off any complaints about the rest of the condo.

Dave understood that most comics are TV addicts who spend a great deal of time channel surfing, looking for their personal gods. Providing an electronic altar eliminated even the most obvious comments such as, "What a dump!" or "Don't you ever clean this place?"

All he heard once he installed the set was, Wow, what a great TV!"

For Dave, who had traded 500 passes with T.C. Electronics for the TV, it was a win-win situation. T.C. Electronics was able to give away the passes during its spring promotion. Dave got the TV and the chance to charge five hundred people four bucks for each glass of fifty-cent wine.

"Nice outfit," Grant said as he looked me up and down.

"Thanks," I said, still embarrassed by my choice of attire.

"Want to watch TV?" Grant asked as he walked to the couch and plopped down. "There's beer in the fridge."

I walked over to the fridge. It was empty except for a carton of milk, one withering carrot, two six-packs of Miller Lite and a couple of Diet Cokes. I grabbed a Diet, pulled back the tab, and walked over and sat down next to Grant.

When I called Grant, I had used the excuse of wanting to ask him about getting ahead in the business, a phrase I'm sure Grant twisted to his own perverted perspective.

"Anything good on?" I asked, taking a large sip, hoping the caffeine in the soda would offset the rum in my system. I had wanted to be loose enough to come to the condo in the first place. Now I wanted to be sober enough to not be tempted to stay.

"This is one of the older Improv reruns. Seinfeld's on it. He was a nobody back then," Grant said as he placed his muscular arm around the back of the couch, directly behind my shoulders.

"Anyone else on it?" I asked, hoping the evening would turn out the way I had planned, not the way Grant did, though I had to admit he was cute. Very, very cute. Why was it that sleaze and muscle often arrived in the same package?

"No one that counts," Cuddler answered. He reached over to the table and picked up a cigar. He clipped the tip and tossed it into an ashtray. The matchbook that he used to light his cigar was from Mystic Lake Casino.

"You've been to Mystic?" I asked, remembering how he had snapped at LaVonne when she suggested going to the casino for fun. The matchbook convinced me that for Grant, casinos were never fun.

"Why don't we turn off the tube?" he asked, using the remote to click off the TV. I detected a little lust as his eyes met mine. Very little, but for Grant, a little was enough.

I was sure that Grant hadn't the slightest romantic interest in me. I was also convinced that it didn't matter to him if he found me attractive. When it came to the possibility of scoring, if he thought she was easy, Grant would be turned on by Janet Reno.

"So, Grant," I said, moving myself one cushion away. "I've been thinking about replacing my agent, Ray Raymond."

"You mean you want one that knows vaudeville's been dead for seventy years?" Grant asked with a smirk as he moved one cushion closer.

"I know Ray's a little strange," I replied defensively. Ray may be a crappy agent, but he's my crappy agent.

I snapped my legs together as Grant put his hand on my plump kneecap. Until Grant placed his hand there, I never knew that was where my G-spot was located.

"A little strange? The man's a dinosaur. Do you know he actually represents a singing dog act?"

"Hey, the Polka Poodles are fun," I told him, fondly remembering them in their little polka-dot skirts and hats.

"Mannie, did you hear what you just said? You've got to get out of this state before you end up telling knock-knock jokes."

"Minnesota's not that bad," I answered, knowing full well that for someone who wants to make it in show business, it is.

The weather alone could kill a career.

"If you want to work fishing resorts all your life, then stay here. Otherwise, get out. I need another beer," Grant said abruptly. He stood up and as he walked away he started to unbutton the front of his black silk shirt. His chest had more hair than a beauty pageant.

I was in trouble. I'm turned on by fur.

Grant went to the fridge. I started going through the magazines on the table, pretending to be scanning them when in reality I was hoping he'd left his wallet underneath the mess. I was here to get into Grant's wallet and nothing else. My old friend and ex-beau, Murray Fischer, was waiting for the information I would give him from Grant's wallet.

Every month dozens of ordinary citizens, like Murray, give stand-up a try. Most of them eventually give up and go back to the real world. I stayed in contact with a few of them, especially those I dated.

Murray tried comedy for a year before he quit trying to get into both show business and my bedroom. He found it easier, though, to break into my boudoir. As I remembered, I eagerly opened the door and pulled him in.

Murray worked as a senior systems analyst for one of the largest and shadiest credit companies located in Minneapolis. His true passion, besides almond-flavored massage oil, was computer hacking.

I hadn't seen Murray for months when I called, but I knew I could ask for his help. What I was requesting was illegal, of course, but legality was never an issue with Murray.

He agreed to help but said it would be easier if I found out Grant's social security or driver's license number.

I went to the condo to accomplish that task. I was determined to get into Grant's pants. And from the looks of it, he was determined to get into mine.

"Mannie," Grant smiled seductively as he leaned over the couch, "let's finish our little talk in the bedroom."

I nodded my head and watched him go into the other room.

I kept telling myself to stay cool. I had to act completely professional, like the private investigator I thought myself to be.

I had to be in absolute control of every emotion, including my sexual desires, which were currently ricocheting off the walls.

When I reached the bedroom door, Grant was waiting for me. He kissed me long and deep.

For the sake of my investigation, I kissed him back. For a very, very long time.

Grant's tongue began to explore places in my mouth that my dentist didn't even know about. For me, if a man is a good kisser, it doesn't matter what else he is.

Grant managed to continue playing Lewis and Clark in my mouth while navigating me toward the bed. As we fell backwards, the bed creaked so loud that we laughed.

"Sort of ruined the moment, eh?" I said, wanting to slow things down a bit as Grant slid his hand under my sweater.

"Not for me," he answered and clamped down once again on my open mouth.

"Do me a favor, Grant," I said, pulling away from him and gasping for air.

"Sure. Anything. I love kinky. Are you kinky, Mannie Grand?"

"In more ways than you'll ever know," I responded. "Would you mind taking a shower," I said, pulling gently on his furry chest.

Grant immediately sat up. The moment was ruined for him. He sniffed underneath both his armpits.

"I took a shower earlier," he said.

"No, that's not it. I just need to check my answering machine and, well, then I'd like to join you in the shower."

"Now, that sounds too good to pass up," Grant smiled as he walked toward the bathroom.

"Wait," I said, already mortified by the words that were going to come from my mouth. I knew I would sound like the biggest pervert in the Twin Cities—or at least Richfield.

"You know how a man refers to himself as either a breast man or a leg man?" I asked Grant.

"I'm both," Grant smiled.

"I'm sure you are," I told him. "See, I'm what you'd call a 'bun' girl. Why don't you let me see that cute little butt of yours

142

as you walk away. Take off your pants but not your underwear. I like my surprises one at a time."

"Mannie Grand, you're the one who's surprising me," Grant chuckled. "I had no idea you were so wicked."

Grant took off his shirt and pants slowly. Like most hunks, he knew his power. I couldn't control my loud sigh as his pants hit the floor. Anything for the investigation.

Grant started singing "Strangers In the Night" as he walked into the bathroom. As soon as I heard the water running I reached for his jeans. His wallet was still in the back pocket.

I rustled through it. Quickly I found both his social security card and driver's license. I picked up a small notebook sitting on the nightstand and wrote down the information I needed, my terror of being discovered gaining momentum with every stroke.

"Mannie," Grant called in a sing-song fashion from the steamy room. "Oh, Mannie."

"I'm coming," I answered. I folded the piece of paper and put it into the back pocket of my skirt.

"Don't come without me," he teased.

Men can be so gooey when they're horny.

I walked to the window that faced the streets and drew open the drapes. I then turned around and started unbuttoning my sweater. I was going to continue with my ruse as long as I had to.

"Mannie?" Grant yelled one more time. "Grab another towel from the hallway closet."

"Sure," I answered, happy for any delay. I opened the closet and grabbed one. The closet was basically bare except for a few cleaning towels and supplies. A sheet of paper was taped on the inside of the door, listing chores for the condo's cleaning crew. Every task was initialed and dated by the person who accomplished it.

I stared at the list for a few seconds longer before I walked into the bathroom, Grant pulled back the shower curtain and smiled a wonderful smile. I swallowed hard and made sure I only looked at his face as I started to unzip my skirt, suddenly there was a loud pounding on the front door.

"Someone's knocking," I said, zipping up.

"Forget about it," Grant said, yanking me toward the shower.

"But it could be important," I told him.

"Forget about it," Grant said again as he pulled me, shoes and all, into the shower with him. The knocking became louder and more persistent as the water soaked me to the skin.

"Maybe we should just see who it is?" I suggested as I stepped out of the shower and handed him his robe. My drenched leather skirt squeaked as I moved.

Grant grudgingly put on his robe and headed out of the bathroom. But instead of walking to the front door, he walked over to the nightstand beside the bed. Although he tried to hide it, I saw him take a gun from the top drawer and put it in the pocket of his robe.

As we walked to the front door, Grant was swearing like Andrew Dice Clay. He looked through the security eye and swore one more time.

He growled as he unbolted the door. "It's your roommate."

"LaVonne?" I asked, acting overly-shocked. "What's she doing here?"

Grant opened the door. LaVonne was standing there breathless.

"Mannie! You've got to come home. It's an emergency!"

"I'll get my coat," I told her.

"And your top," she reminded me.

As I turned, Grant grabbed me by the arm and said to LaVonne, "What emergency?"

"What emergency?" she dumbly repeated. Once in a while, a blonde joke fits her.

"What is so damned important?" Grant asked.

Without losing a beat, LaVonne replied. "The water is running in the kitchen and it won't shut off."

I couldn't believe her idiotic response. Suddenly, she and I were acting like Lucy and Ethel.

"Water's all over the kitchen floor and heading toward the living room," she yelled, as if she were repeating a line from a '50's horror film.

"Did you call the Super?" Grant asked, looking doubtful at LaVonne's tale of woe.

"He's out of town. Mannie, you've got to come quick," she

said with such conviction that, had I not known better, I would have thought she was telling the truth.

"Sorry, Grant," I said, grabbing my coat and tossing it over my saturated body. I joined LaVonne as she raced and I squeaked down the steps.

"Last week, Grant Cuddler once again proved he was the most underrated act in the business. The man's a genius."
Female critic for *The Sun Current* newspapers.

2 4

"That was the best excuse you could come up with?" I asked as I drove home from our little charade.

"Grant caught me off guard," LaVonne answered. "Anything interesting happen?"

"No," I said, keeping my eyes on the road ahead. I didn't want her to see I was lying.

"We only necked a little," I added, as coldly as possible.

"Was he any good?" she asked with a lilt in her voice.

"Damn good," I sighed, LaVonne knows me too well. She knows when I'm attracted to a man even before I know it myself.

We continued the ride in silence. LaVonne fell asleep. I kept going through facts about the murder case in my head. I now thought of myself as its primary investigator.

As I drove back to our apartment, I managed to reach into my pocket and pull out my notebook. It was wet but so far most of the numbers had not run together. I wasn't as careful as I might have been, but then I hadn't expected to take a shower fully dressed.

My adrenaline was still pumping. I was on an incredible high. As I pried into Grant's wallet, every nerve in my body had tingled with fear and anticipation.

I had never felt so alive. For the first time in my life, I realized that stealing was its own reward. I loved every minute of my caper. Perhaps the Grand criminal tendency was an inheritance that I didn't want to refuse.

I pulled up in front of the triplex we lived in and noticed that LaVonne had failed to turn off the lights again. I would have reminded her about it, but she was sound asleep. She woke up when I clicked off the radio, mumbling something about wanting to call in sick to her temp job. We trudged up the three flights to our apartment. As soon as we reached our landing, we stopped dead in our tracks.

"My God," LaVonne said, touching our apartment door, which was hanging wide open halfway off its hinges. I would tell you that our apartment had been broken into but "broken" is too weak a word — it was totally trashed.

The couch was upside down with its bottom was ripped open. All of the cushions were slashed. Our two Salvation Army overstuffed chairs were shredded to the bare lumber frames.

I shuddered. What would have happened if LaVonne or I had been home?

The TV set was lying on the floor, its private innards of wires and circuit boards splayed across the carpet. The stereo speakers, the only things of real value that I owned, were disemboweled, their wiry intestines dangling in mid-air.

Almost every family picture and art print had been pulled off the walls and thrown on the floor. The only picture that was not slashed was LaVonne's high school graduation picture. The rest of our slaughtered possessions looked like they should have chalk marks drawn around them.

We edged our way down the hall and saw that the bathroom's medicine cabinet had been emptied. Bottles of shampoos, conditioners and cough syrups were lying broken on the tile floor, their contents draining slowly into ugly puddles.

We walked down the hallway and peered into our bedrooms. Our mattresses and box springs had been torn apart. The dresser drawers were emptied, their contents in piles. Blouses, jeans, and purses were turned inside out, many of them ripped apart.

The kitchen, too, had been ransacked. The contents of our freezer were lying on the kitchen floor. A half gallon of chocolate ice cream was melting over dozens of semi-frozen fish sticks. Cereal boxes had been emptied. Only one item remained undamaged: the Disneyland gift bucket of holiday popcorn we had received from Lenny and Bob was still sealed in its original factory packaging. The intruder did not bother opening it, perhaps because we never had.

The electric stove was yanked from the wall. Our kitchen

table was upside down. Even the ceiling was vandalized. The light fixtures were broken, only the bare bulbs remained.

"What in the hell were they looking for?" LaVonne cried, her body trembling.

"I don't know," I lied as I dialed 911. "I don't know."

I would have preferred not calling the police. I dreaded letting Brott know that he was right in assuming that I was connected, albeit after the fact, to the murder.

But if I didn't call, LaVonne would insist on knowing why. We both knew our insurance policy required a police report be filed.

Up until that moment, I thought I could get away with not telling LaVonne about the money. It was one thing for me to risk my life, but it was unfair to risk hers.

It was hard to admit that my stupidity had put both our lives in danger.

"Look at this mess!" LaVonne screamed as I hung up the phone, her tears turning to rage. "They've even gutted my stuffed animals. These were no burglars! They were on a mission!"

LaVonne wiped away her tears and glared at me.

"Mannie, I know you've been hiding something from me. Don't you think it's time you tell me what it is?"

In the distance, I heard the cry of sirens. The police were nearing our apartment. I was caught between the proverbial rock and a very, very hard place. I made a decision and hoped, for LaVonne's sake, that it was the right one.

I quickly told her about the money, though I didn't tell her where it was hidden. I told her who I thought had destroyed our apartment. Finally, I told her who I thought had killed Bob.

We had only a few minutes to compose ourselves before the police arrived. After stepping out of the wet clothes I was wearing, I tossed them on the floor. I managed to find a T-shirt and a pair of jeans that were still intact. As I zipped up, we heard Brott's troops marching up the stairs.

Brott and the two policemen who arrived with him did not bother to knock. Why would they? A truck could have driven through our doorway and we wouldn't have noticed.

"What a disaster," Brott said, kicking a shattered crystal vase out of his way as he walked toward us, notebook in hand. "Any idea who did this?"

"None," LaVonne answered with melodramatic intensity. Thank God she's a better comedian than actor.

Brott walked around the kitchen, taking in every inch of the surroundings with his well-trained eyes.

"Where were you when this happened?" he asked.

"We were at The Box," LaVonne said, her voice inflection going up at the end like a California Valley Girl. It sounded more like a question than a response.

"You guys left the club around ten. There's over an hour that's not accounted for," Brott said matter-of-factly, as if it was normal for him to know every aspect of our lives.

I looked at LaVonne. I needed to convey to her that if Brott knew we left the club, then he probably knew where we had gone. This was no time to lie.

"We went to the condo to see Grant Cuddler," I said. "It was business. LaVonne waited outside in the car."

Brott looked me straight in the eye and asked, "Do you think this is connected to Bob?"

Before I could answer, LaVonne said a firm, "No."

"I think a deranged fan did this," I added, praying that LaVonne would follow my line of bullshit and back me up. As usual with best friends, she did.

"There's hundreds of weirdoes that hang out at comedy clubs," LaVonne piped in. "I worked a club in Ohio where the headliner's legs were broken by a drunken heckler."

"Remember the Colorado tour?" I asked LaVonne, hoping she would follow suit. "A psychotic mountain man was stalking female comics."

"Read the tabloids," LaVonne told Brott. "Every star has at least one stalker. To the residents of Bottineau, North Dakota, Mannie and I are the closest thing to Hollywood they'll ever see."

"At least you can't blame this on Charley," I said to Brott, wanting to remind him of the innocent man he'd locked behind bars.

149

"Maybe there's no one to blame," Brott responded sarcastically.

It took a few seconds for it to sink in that Brott was implying that we'd devastated our own apartment.

"Jesus Christ," I yelled, "Are you insane? Why would we destroy everything we own?"

"I have no idea, but I look at every angle. I'm a cop, remember?"

"How could I forget?" I said with such anger that Brott turned his face away from me. If LaVonne was right that Brott was attracted to me, he was doing everything he could to hide it.

"I don't want the two of you staying here tonight," Brott said. "This is now an official police investigation site."

"And when you find my fingerprints, on *my* stuff, in *my* apartment, am I going to get *my* ass thrown in jail?" I screamed at him.

Like a patient mom trying to calm a tyrannical three-year-old, LaVonne started patting me on my back.

"Do you two have a place to stay?" he asked, not even acknowledging my sarcasm.

"Yes," I said in disgust.

"Is it safe?" Brott asked.

"Yes," I answered, taking one final glance at the destruction and debris scattered around my home. "Safe enough."

I knew of only one place to go. I had made so many mistakes in the last few days that I hoped I was not making another one in choosing where LaVonne and I would spend the night.

One thing I knew for sure was — he had a big gun.

"A year after we divorced, my ex-husband sent me a ring with a note reading, "This is an ex-anniversary ring. It means I'd divorce you all over again." Mannie Grand, Polka & Laughs, Crivitz, Wisconsin.

25

Grant was gracious when LaVonne and I showed up at his door, asking for refuge. He saw how bone tired and upset we were and led us to the second bedroom, without even trying to join us. LaVonne and I slept for eleven straight hours.

By five p.m. LaVonne was making a pot of coffee while I showered. As I felt the water cascade down my body, I remembered being in the same shower with Grant only the night before. I had been fully clothed, soaking wet, terrified that he'd find out that I had gone through his wallet, and loving every minute of it.

When I become involved with a man — which I always find it better not to do — I vacillate between being unconditionally loving and maniacally critical. But then, ever since my brief marriage to one roving-eye comic, I've never trusted men. I discovered my ex-husband in bed with another female comic. It was easy to locate him at the time. We were on our honeymoon.

My attraction to Grant was as strong as when I fell head over heels in love with my ex. I had a combination of intense sexual attraction to Grant's charm, combined with a major revulsion to his faults. I did not understand how he could, at a moment's notice, be so cynical, yet, in the next moment, be nothing less than enchanting.

I was aware of my schizophrenic personality when it came to romance. I knew I wasn't in love with Grant. I also knew I was attracted to Brott. I always found myself drawn to at least two men. Being attracted to one would have been too scary for me. One man hinted at commitment, two meant fun and games.

But this was a love triangle I could never have imagined: a

151

potential murderer, a cop who thought I could be the killer, and me — innocent as a wolf in plus-size sheep's clothing.

I no longer thought Grant killed Bob, but I knew he was somehow connected. I was convinced that he was set up as the fall guy to take the rap. With a little bit of luck, and my friend Murray's help, I would prove my theory.

I pulled Grant's white terrycloth robe off a hook and wrapped myself in it. I felt safe inside it, pulling it gently around me. I wondered if I would have felt just as safe with Grant inside of me.

I left the bathroom and opened the nightstand drawer to look for the Yellow Pages. I needed to make a few calls. Except for the directory, the drawer was empty. The gun was not in it.

LaVonne yelled from the kitchen, "There's no cream!"

She usually puts half a cup of cream and a fourth of a cup of sugar in every mug of coffee.

"Try it black for a change," I said as I entered the small kitchen. "See if there is any of the powdered stuff in the cabinets."

She opened the door and found three jars of fake dried cream, all of which had been opened and left, no doubt, by touring comedians.

"Which do you think is the newest one?" she asked.

"The one that's the least green," I responded. "Do you know where Grant went?"

"He said he had to meet someone. Do you think he knows you have the million dollars?"

"Maybe," I answered.

I grabbed a slice of the deep-dish pizza that LaVonne had ordered for our dinner-time breakfast. She put the coffee thermos on the table and I poured myself a large cup. I needed all the energy I could get.

"What time will you be at the club?" I asked her as I sprinkled extra salt on my slice of pizza.

"The usual, " she said, "a half hour before show time. Are you coming?"

"No. How about meeting me at Perkins at two a.m."

"Sure. I called Dave while you were in the shower. Both

shows are sold out," she said, grabbing another slice.

"Blood sports always draw," I reminded her. "Maybe everyone's hoping someone else will get killed. Did you call our insurance agent?"

"Yes," LaVonne sighed. "And so did the police. What will we do if the insurance company says we did it?"

"Being charged with fraud is the least of my worries," I told her. "At least that's not a hanging offense."

"They don't hang anyone anymore, do they?" LaVonne asked, her face filled with concern. LaVonne is to the left of left politically. She has even worn a T-shirt that reads 'Liberal and Proud of It!' to a Rush Limbaugh appearance.

"That was just a figure of speech, LaVonne. No one's going to hang. Did you manage to get enough clothes from our apartment?"

"Not really," she said, "but I called my sister. She's bringing over a few things. She's also giving you a couple of outfits."

"How could your sister possibly have clothes that are my size?" I asked, knowing that she's even smaller than LaVonne.

"She's bringing her husband's."

"Beggars can't be choosers," I said, wondering how I would look in Ernie's clothes. He worked as a mechanic and loved to bowl and play softball. Whatever I wore would have the name "Ernie" embroidered over my left breast.

I finished eating my high cholesterol, high sodium breakfast and left the table. I needed to get dressed and out of there.

The condo's second bedroom had twin beds. LaVonne had already made hers, and I, being true to myself, did not make mine. I'm convinced that in my last life, I was rich and had dozens of servants doing all the menial chores, like cooking and cleaning, that in this life I routinely refuse to do. But today I couldn't afford to be a slacker. There were things I both had to do and undo.

The first was to call Murray and ask him to wait for me outside of Dekka Credit. Next, I called Milos' and hung up when I heard Lenny's voice. I didn't want to talk to Lenny, not yet. Later, I would talk to Dave at the club. Finally, I would locate Milos the Shit.

As I headed back to the kitchen, fully dressed, my tension returned when I realized that I had to leave this comfortable haven. I grabbed one more slice of pizza and headed for the door.

"Where are you going?" LaVonne asked in a worried voice. She tried not to pry too much, knowing that if she did, I'd shut down even more.

"The less you know, the better," I said, not wanting to get her any more involved than she already was.

She paused a minute before she snapped.

"Damn you, Mannie! You're keeping me in the dark! You ever think maybe I could help? Maybe even do a better job than you?"

"Well, I...," I smiled and stammered.

"Don't you realize that Bob, who was my friend too, is dead — forever — and that Charley's in jail — maybe forever — and our apartment looks like the movie set of *Twister?*"

"Don't forget to add our lives are in danger," I joked weakly, hoping to ease her fears.

It didn't work.

"Do I have to remind you," LaVonne continued, "that you are a forty-one-year-old underpaid and underrated comedian, not a detective? I've been thinking about it, and I've decided to tell Brott everything."

"You can't," I whispered, my voice refusing to leave my throat.

"And why not?" she yelled, her gentle demeanor transformed into that of a raging bull.

"Because," I said, as I grabbed my coat and headed for the door. "I haven't told you everything."

I could hear LaVonne yelling as I ran down the condo steps, "Dammit, Mannie! You're going to get us killed! What are you hiding?"

The most obvious answer was, of course, a million bucks. But then LaVonne, who excelled in subterfuge and understatement, often missed the obvious. With all the questions she had asked, she had failed to ask where I stashed the dough, and I, of course, didn't bother to tell her.

And, except for every other minute, I rarely thought about it myself. Unless, of course, snowflakes started to fall or the wind started to blow. Then I'd think that maybe I wasn't as clever as I thought I was in choosing such a public place.

But as I looked at the city around me and saw thousands of buildings surrounded by deep snow, I thought, where would someone even begin to look? And why would they think of looking for it outdoors? Especially in Minnesota, with temperatures hovering well-below zero, the air could be so frigid that your lungs felt like they were being pierced by an ice-pick every time you breathed.

No one thought of going outside in Minnesota in winter — no one — except for the thousands of fanatic winter-loving Minnesotans that I never think about. People who deliberately go out to play in the snow, slide down hills, skate, and ice fish. Those folks.

Focused on trying to find the killer, I had totally forgotten about the local Festival of Frozen Fools, St. Paul's Winter Carnival. It's an annual celebration of the un-celebrateable — a tribute to ice and snow. There are parades, dances, beauty contests and a fifty-foot palace made from ice.

The highlight of the event is always a treasure hunt. A small medallion, about the circumference of a bagel, is hidden somewhere in the park's thick blanket of ice and snow. Whoever finds the medallion would receives thousands of dollars in prize money.

Each day, the St. Paul Pioneer Press prints a single clue to the medallion's location. The first clue is always so obscure that few, if any, could decipher it. The second is a bit clearer. By the end of the week, when the final and most obvious clue is announced, mobs of people arrive with snow shovels at the then easily recognizable location.

I had hidden Bob's considerably larger treasure not in St. Paul but its sister city, Minneapolis. I prayed that Minneapolis and St. Paul would continue their rivalry and that the medallion would not be hidden west of the Mississippi for the first time in history.

After my screaming match with LaVonne, I sat in front of the condo in my car. It took a few minutes before I was calm enough to turn the ignition. Once again it miraculously started. I don't know what it is about Minnesota cars, but against all odds, they continue to work.

Perhaps they just adjust to the frigid climate like the rest of us, chugging along while praying for spring. Or maybe my car always started because of the plastic Virgin Mary statue LaVonne had duct-taped to the dashboard. LaVonne had even put a tiny muffler and hat on Our Lady of the Battery.

It took ten minutes before the car was semi-warm and the windows were halfway defrosted. It would have been comfortable to wait inside until the car was driveable, but I refused. I would rather have frozen my ample buns off than deal with LaVonne's anger.

I tallied up our financial losses. Our furniture and books would cost, even if we bought them used, at least two grand. The electronics would be another deuce. The really important stuff, like the Partridge Family Lava Lamp and my original Mystery Date Game, were irreplaceable.

So far, my amateur sleuthing had cost us over $4,000. Then there was the additional problem of my expense account — the ten thousand dollars I had liberated to help with my investigation.

I understood that stoolies and rats aren't cheap. I found out that friends aren't either. My old bud, Murray, was getting half of the expense money I had left.

I could barely see out the front window of my car when I said "good enough" and pulled into traffic. I didn't bother to turn on the cassette player. Not even the mind numbing Abba could comfort me. I kept looking in the mirror. For no reason, I had the odd feeling I was being followed.

"Don't be paranoid," I reminded myself, knowing I have the tendency to make mole hills into the Rocky Mountains.

I headed into downtown Minneapolis to Hennepin and First. Dekka Credit was located a few blocks north in the warehouse district.

The area had been taken over by trendy bistros and vegetarian restaurants featuring Cajun tofu and meatless meatloaf. A few of the run-down buildings had become artists' lofts. Massage parlors and sex shops dotted the landscape as a reminder that, trendy or not, it was still a city.

Dekka was at the far end of the district and sat directly over Leather Expressions. Expressions did not sell luggage or cheap Italian furniture. Specializing in promoting a lifestyle of bondage and submission, its inventory consisted mainly of full-face masks and studded whips. I was not comforted knowing that if I were to scream while upstairs at Dekka, no one except the gleefully bound and gagged folks downstairs would hear me and they would be envious.

I pulled into the alley behind the building. Dumpsters overflowed with shredded credit reports and discarded sex shop items. Murray once told me that the waste cans held enough information to ruin one out of every two Minnesotans.

He was waiting for me at the bottom of the wooden stairwell that led upstairs to his office. He was chewing tobacco because even though Dekka sat over an S&M emporium, it was nicotine-free.

Murray spat out his chew and waved at me as I stepped out of my car. I noticed he hadn't shaved off his beard. I could see black curly chest hair protruding out of his shirt. Murray was the hairiest man I had ever known. I was as comfortable as a bug in a rug when he used to hold me.

He liked to brag that he was a nicotine addict who was twenty pounds overweight. Having exercised once in the '80s, and not liking it, he bragged that he would "die young and leave a bad body."

Yet, as I remembered, it wasn't that bad.

"Hi ya, babe," he said in his macho way, trying to conceal the fact that he is basically a computer nerd.

"It's good to see you," I told him as I slid four thousand dollars into his pants pocket.

"It's better to see you," he snorted as we walked up the icy steps.

157

"I'm the only one on night shift, babe," he continued. "We'll have the place to ourselves."

I felt his rather large hand tracing my rather large butt. Like death and taxes, Murray's enormous sexual appetite could be counted on.

He unlocked Dekka's back door, and we walked down a dark and narrow hallway to the main computer room.

"Did you bring the information?" he asked, as he sat down at a terminal.

The walls surrounding his desk were covered in baseball memorabilia featuring the Minnesota Twins. There was, however, a large calendar that featured a teddy bear as its centerfold. A bold feminine signature flowed across the bottom. A series of carefully drawn hearts with happy faces encircled her name. I assumed the calendar was a gift from someone who, like me, knew the pleasure of cuddling with such a furry creature.

I fished the paper with the needed numbers out of my jeans pocket and handed it to Murray. After last night's watery fiasco, I was lucky to be missing only the last two digits. Murray said the missing figures were not a problem and that the computer could easily compensate. He began to download the information and we sat back and waited.

"If I give you another name and approximate birthplace and year, can you come up with anything?" I asked, as we waited for the computer to do its magic.

"I can try," he said, with a cocky smile that told me that he could.

I grabbed a scratch pad and wrote out the information. When Murray saw the name I had written, he shook his head in disbelief but didn't say a word.

It took approximately three minutes for Grant's entire life to flash on the screen in front of us. The first thing I saw was that Grant had been lying about his age. He was three years older than he said.

Grant earned approximately forty thousand dollars a year — a far cry from the heyday of comedy when he, like most headliners, was earning a quarter of a million dollars annually.

He was over the limit on every one of his credit cards.

American Express had canceled his account. There was a lien on his condo. By the looks of it, Grant was in deep financial shit.

I asked Murray if it was possible to look at the individual charges on Grant's credit cards from his computer system. He nodded, and with one muffled phone call and four minutes worth of computer commands, proceeded to do so.

Virtually every charge or cash advance originated where I thought they would — Las Vegas. I could tell by just glancing at the charges how different Grant and I were. Not one of the charges was for the all-you-can-eat buffets.

I watched Murray navigate the keyboard, painfully aware that he possessed the ability not only to investigate an individual's life but, with the right commands, to destroy it.

No one is us, I thought. Everything about everyone is stored in electronic memory somewhere, just floating in cyber-space, waiting to be accessed.

I didn't know what disturbed me more, the invasion of privacy that is possible or that, this time, I was the one doing the invading. This was nothing less than a high-tech invasion of Grant's secret life.

I wished there was another way.

Murray printed out the information on the screen and handed the page to me. I carefully folded it in quarters and put it in my pocket. He entered the second name and, once again, we sat back and waited. I noticed that Murray placed his hand on my knee and I noticed that I didn't remove it.

The credit report and history flashed on the screen. I scanned it quickly and confirmed what I had suspected all along.

"Thanks, Murray," I told him. "Can you print out this information for me?"

"Sure," he said reaching toward the keyboard. At that exact moment the lights went out.

"Goddamnit," he said, mildly irritated. "The damn power supply in this building is so damn weak that every time they turn on a vibrator downstairs, it...."

He stopped talking when he heard footsteps and mumbled voices on the stairs.

The power supply was fine. We weren't.

"I had a feeling I was being followed," I whispered, "but I dismissed it as paranoia."

"Now you tell me," Murray responded.

We saw a small beam of light shine down the corridor and heard footsteps coming down the hallway. Murray jumped up and locked the door. He slid a file cabinet in front of it. He signaled for me to open the window. I ran over, lifted it and saw that it was a two-story drop into a closed dumpster.

"I can't jump," I told him.

"You don't have to," he said as he forced me to the floor. "Do what I say, Mannie, and for once in your life, shut up."

If he hadn't been trying to save my life, I would have been pissed. I crept along on my hands and knees, my heart pumping with pure adrenaline.

Murray crawled around the back of the Specter 5500 mainframe computer. It sat on a raised platform that allowed technicians limited access to its underside through a work panel located at the bottom.

Murray carefully slid back the panel and told me to slide underneath the computer. It's access area was 24 inches high and I quickly found out that, on my back, I was 23 inches tall. Murray quickly slid in on his back after me, and with his left hand he closed the work panel. With any luck and no sneezes the intruder wouldn't figure out that two terrified souls were lying underneath the platform, crammed together like sardines in a high-tech coffin.

We heard the file cabinet crash to the floor as the door was kicked in. I gasped when it fell. Murray reached over to cover my mouth, but couldn't. His arm had become entwined in wires and cables.

Footsteps began to circle the computer. We counted on the workstation entrance panel being invisible to the untrained eye. I heard our invader walk toward the window. For the next six seconds there was nothing but terrifying silence and then...

Five loud pops in a row. July 4th was months away so unless someone was celebrating early, it was not firecrackers. I'd watched enough James Bond movies to know what a semi-automatic sounded like.

We hoped our intruder would assume that we jumped out of the window and ran down the alley. Now I was praying that whoever was unfortunate enough to be walking by in the alley was still alive.

I heard the intruder run out of the room and down the hallway. Murray and I did not move an inch. We couldn't. We were stuck. The emergency latch on the side had activated. We were locked in. The only thing we could do was wait in the dark until the morning shift arrived.

"I just heard that to be a successful and highly paid executive, you must learn to play golf. Now I know why my last promotion was so small, I only play miniature golf." Murray Fischer, Open Mike Night at The Comedy Box, the only good joke he had.

26

LaVonne panicked when I didn't show up to meet her at Perkins. She had no way of knowing that I was perfectly safe, resting underneath a ton and a half of steel and circuitry, scrunched next to 210 pounds of pulsating testosterone. She not only notified Brott of my mysterious disappearance but also the media.

LaVonne is a lifelong chum with a news personality on Channel 11. They belonged to the same Girl Scout troop and, while in high school, dated the same football team. LaVonne dated one half, while the newscaster dated the other.

By five a.m., with still no word from me and no assurances from Brott that I could be found, LaVonne called her friend and told her I was missing. She also said it had to be connected to Bob Patterson's murder and that Charley, the man the police had arrested, had been framed.

Since it was a slow news day, I was the lead story on its 6 a.m. newscast. KARE 11 had my face plastered across its broadcast. When I arrived back at the condo at 8:45 and opened the door, I saw LaVonne sobbing in front of the television, staring at my photo and listening to the words, "Minnesota's Funny Lady, Mannie Grand, is missing and feared dead."

I immediately knew that LaVonne had called her friends at the station. We yelled at each other for a few minutes before we realized the absurdity of the situation and started to laugh. LaVonne relished my tale of being trapped with the perpetually horny Murray, whose last meal had to have been a bowl of garlic sautéed with anchovies.

In between our chuckling, we watched the news report and I managed to ask her where Grant was.

"He's sleeping like a pet rock," she told me.

"Some protector," I sighed, and we started laughing again.

We were laughing at anything and everything, even the unfunny. Our pressure valves were ready to blow and the only way we knew to let off steam was to act like idiots.

The phone rang and I picked it up, still laughing. I was amazed at how quickly I stopped being amused.

"I'm perfectly fine," I said to Dad, as I clicked through the channels and saw my face being flashed on every station in town.

I continued channel surfing as Dad ranted on how I needed to take better care of myself. Channel 5's caption read "Local Comedian — Dead or Alive?"

"I'll call the stations to let them know I'm safe," I promised. I didn't tell Dad that I planned to wait a while before I did. This was the most publicity I'd ever had.

"Where were you last night?" he asked. "You didn't stay overnight at some man's apartment, did you?"

Like all dads, he still thought of me as his little girl. He was convinced that a big bad wolf was at my door. He didn't know the wolf's name was Murray.

"I didn't spend the night at anyone's apartment," I told him honestly.

On the night our apartment was vandalized, I had given Dad the condo's telephone number. He wanted us to stay with him, but I didn't want to get him involved. I forgot that, because I am his daughter, he was already involved. He had been asking if there was anything he could do to help.

Up until then, I told him no.

"Dad, there is something you can do for me," I said to him, as I walked into the other room so LaVonne couldn't hear. "Do you still have friends in Vegas?"

"Sure," he said, immediately changing from Dad the Protector to the father I was more familiar with — a fellow compulsive gambler.

"You wanna go to Las Vegas, Mannie?" he asked excitedly.

"We could hop the Northwest daily. We'll stay downtown. I've never liked the strip. We can..."

"I don't want to go to Vegas, Dad. Remember? I don't gamble, anymore, " I told him. At least not with money. "I need you to check on someone for me."

"Sure," he said, "I could do that. I could make a few phone calls, except it's always easier to get answers in person."

I looked at the clock and saw that it was 9:15. I knew there was a flight to Vegas at eleven because Dad mentioned it whenever we had lunch together.

"That's the daily flight to Lost Wages, Nevada," he'd say wistfully when he heard the plane flying overhead.

I envisioned him in Vegas. He would be acting twenty years younger. He wouldn't need his cane. If he did use it, it would only be to push people away from his favorite craps table to make room for himself. Dad hadn't been able to afford to go to Vegas in twelve years. I didn't know when, or if, he'd have another chance.

"Tell ya what, Dad, I've got a little money put away — well, a lot of money actually."

I told Dad who I thought had killed Bob and about the million I had hidden away and where it was. I told him that if something happened, to call Detective Brott and tell them about the money. I told Dad I didn't want anyone else to be killed. If the police had the money, the killing would stop.

I told him that I was sending LaVonne over with an envelope containing fifteen hundred dollars. I had enough of the ten thousand left to cover his flight and hotel room and provide him with a little gambling stake on the side.

I reminded him that I was giving him the money to get answers to my questions and that I needed those answers before he gambled one nickel.

"I don't want you to touch one slot machine before you call me," I told him,

"I won't, Mannie," he assured me, his voice already taking on the sound of heightened anticipation that addicts get. "Not even a penny in the penny slots at the Plaza. You know you can trust me."

I knew I could. Dad might be a compulsive gambler but he's my dad first.

He'd never lied to me. Of course, he never had a million reasons to do so before.

I reminded him to call Northwest Airlines as soon as he hung up. He told me he'd be staying at the Fremont.

"The Fremont's got a history," he informed me. "It's not sterile like those new fancy-shmancy places."

I'd given my dad crummy Father's Day presents for years. The trip to Vegas, courtesy of Bob's killers, would hopefully make up for it.

He hung up the phone and I relaxed. I'd gotten rid of a third of my worries. Dad would be safely out of town. Now I only needed to get rid of LaVonne and Grant. I wanted them out of the condo by noon.

"LaVonne, have you eaten breakfast yet?" I asked as I walked back into the kitchen, carrying an envelope that I had just stuffed with the money I was giving Dad.

"Not yet," she answered.

"I need you to get this envelope to my father within twenty minutes. Can you do that?"

"Sure," she answered. She must have trusted me again because she didn't ask why.

"I want you and Grant to stay away for a while," I said firmly. My voice made it clear that I wouldn't backpedal on this one.

"What's a while?" she asked. I could see her eyes cloud over again with worry.

She wasn't half as worried as I was.

"Until tomorrow morning," I told her, knowing that by then everything would have fallen into place — one way or another. And if the person I expected to show up at the condo went ballistic on me, then at least she and Grant would be safe.

"I've reserved a suite at the downtown Radisson," I told her. "Do you know when Grant went to bed?"

"I haven't seen him since last night's show. I got in at three and just assumed he was asleep."

I walked to the master bedroom and knocked gently and then

165

very loudly on the door.

I opened the door, part of me hoping that he'd had the foresight to sleep in pajamas. I didn't see any pajamas. In fact I didn't see anything.

"Grant's not here," I yelled to LaVonne.

I looked around at the room. The bed was meticulously made. On the dresser, combs and brushes were neatly placed in a row. Three cans of male hair spray and oil waited like toy soldiers. Everything was in its place except for Grant.

I leaned for a few seconds against the wall, reminding myself to calm down, to breathe deeply. My chest started aching and sweat started seeping through my clothes. I gathered what strength I had left and forced myself to walk upright, with my shoulders back, and my head held high.

"He didn't come home last night," I told her as I entered the kitchen, faking my composure.

"Maybe he got lucky?" she asked weakly, suggesting that Grant had managed to score.

"No one's that lucky," I told her and then sighed deeply before I added, "Guess what I have to do."

"What?" she asked, her voice trembling a bit. She wasn't buying my serenity act.

"Call Brott and report another missing person."

"It hasn't been twenty-four hours. Brott won't take you seriously."

"I can't wait that long. If I do, Grant won't be missing."

"What do you mean?" she asked.

"He'll be dead."

"I'm a pretty tough broad. My high-school friends names were Killer, Scarface, and Meathook — and they were the cheerleaders." Mannie Grand, Belly Laughs Bar, Moorhead, Minnesota.

27

Once again, LaVonne was right about Brott's asinine insistence on following police procedure to the letter. When I called Brott and told him about Grant, he said we'd have to wait the necessary 24 hours before filing a missing person's report.

"Besides," he said with a sarcastic tone in his voice, "Grant's probably spending the night at some broad's place."

I asked Brott if I could at least come down to the station to start filling out forms for a missing person's report. He hedged until I told him I knew who killed Bob. He told me to come down as soon as possible. I told him I'd be there in a couple of hours; I needed to talk with someone first. I hung up before he could convince me otherwise.

The real villains had begun tumbling into place when Grant asked me to grab a towel from the linen closet. Posted on the inside of the door was a list of cleaning chores. It contained specific instructions, such as "sweep the floor" and "wash the sink." Each job was initialed and dated, as if the crew were kindergartners and had to be held accountable.

The only people I knew that had to be told so precisely what to do, besides toddlers, were comedians. The initials next to each instruction told me I was right. The last entry had jolted me to a painful realization. I verified it the next morning by talking to Dave.

I woke Dave up when I called. I almost laughed when I heard his heavy gold ID bracelet clinking into the mouthpiece. I could tell he'd worn his half dozen rings and chains to bed. I was surprised he didn't sleep with his Mercedes.

I told Dave that I was broke. He started coughing and saying

167

he had to go until I asked him if he had any odd jobs that I could do. Did he still hire comics to clean the condo?

There was a pause and then he said he recently lost one of the two men that had been cleaning the condo for years.

Dave kept his cleaning staff's names confidential. He knew that every comedian wanted to be thought of as a star, not the Tidy Bowl guy.

Yet the job did have its perks. The real payoff came in being at the condo when the headliner arrived.

The comic/cleaner would immediately brown-nose the headliner, asking if he or she needed anything from the grocery store, or needed to be shown around town. They'd offer to do anything at all, and they usually meant "anything."

If all went well, by the end of the week, the lowly cleaner/comic and the headliner would be buds. And your buds can make you a star.

Kissing butt is the name of the game. In a few minutes, I had a feeling that the condo's current scrubbing jokester was going to be kissing mine.

While I waited, I flipped on the TV. I turned to a rerun of "The Andy Griffith Show." It was my favorite episode. Aunt Bea wanted an embroidered bed jacket for her birthday and Andy gave her canning jars instead. That episode always makes me cry. It also makes me realize how totally unprepared I am for life. If I can't handle disappointment in Mayberry, how can I handle the real world?

Finally, there was a light knock on the door, followed a few seconds later by the sound of the door being unlocked. The cleaner came in, carrying a vacuum cleaner and a bucket of rags. He was dressed in old jeans and a ripped T-shirt with Goofy imprinted on the front. Goofy was smiling. Lenny was not.

"Mannie, what are you doing here? Hey, are you and Grant...." Lenny asked, trying to act happy to see me.

"I'm staying here for a few days. My apartment was broken into two nights ago."

"No way," he said as walked over to the sink and filled the bucket with hot water.

"Did they take anything?" he asked quietly.

"You know," I said in a sarcastic Chicago tone, mimicking Lenny's accent, "they took everything, including my trust."

He opened a bottle of pine cleaner, poured a capful into the bucket, and set it on the floor. Except for the lonely sound of the rag mop going back and forth across the black and white vinyl, it was silent.

The night our apartment was vandalized, everything that could possibly be pried or ripped open was, except for one item — the five gallon-gift tin of caramel popcorn that he had given us for Christmas. The original shrink wrap still covered the tin. Lenny was the only one who knew the money could not possibly be inside. He and Bob were the ones who gave us the tin in the first place.

"Are you going to tell me why?" I asked him finally.

"Are you implying that I had something to do with the break-in?" he asked. He kept mopping for a few more minutes and then stopped, leaning his body wearily against the kitchen counter. He switched to an Irish brogue. "We're friends, for God's sake, Mannie me'girl, friends."

I wasn't buying his lies.

"If you wanted to know where the money was, why didn't you just ask me?"

Lenny's normally rose-colored cheeks turned white, making his narrow features seem to melt into each other. He stopped breathing for a few seconds before he spoke again.

"Then you do have it?" Lenny's face hardened as he spoke, his face changing so much it was difficult to recognize him. He certainly wasn't the charming hint of Ireland he used to be.

"I know where it is," I told him, reaching into my pocket to make sure the can of Mace was still there.

Lenny walked over to the sofa and plopped himself down. He let go a troubled sigh of relief. His face softened. The demon Greed must have left his body.

"Do you mind if I smoke?" he asked politely.

I couldn't believe he was asking me what he could or could not do. Why didn't he call me a few days earlier and ask if I minded if he destroyed my life?

"Feel free," I answered.

Lenny pulled out a pack of generic cigarettes, lit one cigarette and inhaled deeply. With his left hand, he tapped on the arm of the couch in a pattern of one, two, three, one, two, three, one, two, three. Lenny was close to drifting off into a hypnotic state, as if somehow he could escape from all of this.

"Where did the money come from?" I demanded, wondering if my theory of its origin was correct.

"A leprechaun gave me his pot o' gold," he joked weakly.

"Dammit, Lenny," I screamed, furious that he was taking it all so calmly. "Is it drug money? A bank heist? What?"

"You know, I don't really know, Mannie," he told me, flicking an ash on the carpet. "What I do know is that some very nasty people want it back."

"I've noticed," I said, clenching my jaw in anger. It was taking every bit of reserve I had not to reach over and start wringing his neck.

"I did you a favor by getting them to search your apartment instead of asking you in person about the money," he said matter-of-factly, almost as if he were proud of such a ludicrous statement.

"Gee, thanks," I told him, feeling hatred for my old friend.

"Trust me," he said, as if that was still a possibility. "It was better that way. When those people ask a question, they don't give you a chance to answer."

"Didn't Bob tell you he asked me to pick it up?" I asked.

"No. By the way, did you know what you were picking up a million dollars?"

"Of course not. If I had known, I wouldn't have done it," I told him, not knowing if that was really true. The last few days had shown me my character traits were not as pure as I had always thought they were. I don't know what I would have done if I had known I could get my hands on a million bucks.

"Tell me what happened the last time you and Bob were here to clean."

I knew from the list in the hallway closet that both of them had been cleaning that day, not just Bob. Each had initialed various jobs they had completed. Bob wasn't alone when he found the money.

"It was Bob's turn to clean that day, but he was running behind schedule," Lenny began. "The previous headliner took his time getting the hell out that morning."

"You're talking about Tom Dilbert?"

"Right. Neither one of us starts to clean until the comics check out. They're supposed to call us and let us know when to come over. Dilbert didn't leave until noon. Grant was scheduled to arrive around one o'clock."

"So you volunteered to help."

"Yeah, it was no big deal. The same old, same old."

"Except this time you found more than dirt."

"I was the one who found the bag of money under the kitchen sink," Lenny said. "I had no idea what was in it. I was just about to open it when Grant and Dave walked through the door."

"What did they say?"

"Dave started immediately bitching about how comics forgot shit all the time and how he always had to pay to ship it somewhere. Grant told him not to worry. He said the bag belonged to Dilbert and he'd get it to him."

"How did Grant know whose bag it was?"

"Grant and Dilbert were friends. He said Dilbert had called him on his cell phone to tell him he had forgotten it. Dilbert asked Grant to get the bag to Duluth."

"I didn't know Dilbert was Grant's friend."

"Dilbert liked to pretend he was everybody's friend."

Tom Dilbert was one of the friendliest and funniest magicians on the comedy club circuit. He was a household name on the West Coast. In fact, he was so loved there that I wondered why he worked Minnesota. Now I was beginning to understand.

"How did Grant get the two of you to drive to Duluth?"

"After Dave left, Grant, Bob and I spent part of the afternoon getting stoned. Pretty soon Bob volunteered the two of us to drive the bag up north."

"You had no idea what was in it?" I asked him.

"We had no idea there was a million bucks in it. Grant hinted that the bag contained a little dope and Tom's promo shit. I had no reason to believe otherwise. I didn't find out what was in it

171

until we checked into the motel."

"Bob didn't tell me you were with him," I said, surprised that I hadn't put that little fact in place myself. Bob was phobic about driving and usually rode the bus. I never even questioned the fact that he said he drove to Duluth to perform an unpaid, ten-minute guest set.

"You gotta understand, I jumped at the chance to go to Duluth," Lenny continued. "I've never been able to get my foot in the door at that club. I thought if I did their headliner a favor, I'd be in."

"Is that why Bob did it?"

"No. He did it for Dilbert."

"Why?" I asked.

"Like I said," Lenny continued, "Dilbert was everybody's friend or at least he liked to keep everyone indebted to him. Bob owed him big-time. Fifteen years ago, Bob was busted in Seattle. He was up on a felony charge for possession."

"How did Dilbert get involved?"

"Supposedly, Dilbert pulled a few strings, a lot of dough was passed, and Bob got off with a warning."

"And forever in Dilbert's debt. What happened in Duluth?" I asked.

"By the time Bob and I got to Duluth, it had started to snow. We decided to spend the night rather than drive back in a storm. My tires were too bald to take the chance. We checked into a cheesy motel on the outskirts of town."

"The Twin Pines?"

Lenny nodded his head. "We planned on giving the bag to Dilbert later on, when we showed up at the club. We didn't even call him to let him know we'd arrived."

"How did you open the duffel bag? There was a lock on it."

"It was just a cheap combination lock. Bob figured it out in a few seconds. That was one of the few tricks he still remembered from his days as a magician."

"He was a magician?" I asked, shocked that clumsy Bob had ever attempted such a difficult art.

"He didn't try magic for long. He was terrible. The only thing he could do well at all was figure out locks."

"If you didn't know the money was in the bag, what were you looking for?" I asked. Even after all that had happened, neither one of them seemed like a thief to me.

"Marijuana, but all we found were a few joints, some of Tom Dilbert's odds and ends and a million bucks."

"And you never gave the bag back to Dilbert?" I asked, shocked at their stupidity. Didn't they think that Dilbert, or somebody, would come looking for it?

"Who could we give it to? Tom had already died in the accident."

"I don't think it was an accident," I told Lenny.

The Pioneer Press had reported that Dilbert's car skidded over a snowpacked embankment into Lake Superior. An especially easy trick if, according to my little theory, a car or truck was pushing Dilbert's auto into the lake.

Lenny's body sank deeper into the sofa cushions. "If I hadn't been so damned greedy, both Bob and Dilbert would still be alive."

"Bob didn't want to keep it?" I asked, glad that at least Bob had a sense of morality.

"Not as much as I did. I convinced Bob it was drug money. At least we'd do good things with it."

"Like what?" I asked, remembering my own get-rich-quick fantasies.

"We'd buy thousands of toys to give Toys for Tots. We'd move to South America and open our own comedy club. We'd invite all our friends to work it. We'd pay them well, too, just like the old days. We were going to have you headline the first week," Lenny laughed, shaking his head in disbelief that he could have been so stupid.

"Didn't you think anyone would be suspicious of the two of you?" I asked, knowing that nothing can make a person stupid as quickly as greed.

"You know, that was our problem, We didn't bother to think," Lenny admitted. "We were high on grass and possibilities. We had valid passports. As far as I was concerned, we could have caught a plane that night and left everything behind."

"And Bob agreed?"

"For about twenty minutes, before he came to his senses and refused. He wanted to drop off the money at the club like we were supposed to and forget the whole thing."

"Why didn't you?"

"I was the driver, remember? I was the one with the car keys. Bob was going only where I wanted him to go."

"Why did you forget the money at the motel? Were you that high?"

"We didn't forget it. Bob left it on purpose. I thought Bob had put the bag into the trunk like I had told him to. He must have hidden it under the bed when I went to the lobby to check out. He didn't tell me what he'd done until we got back to Minneapolis."

My throat tightened: I was afraid to ask the next question. "What happened when he told you?"

"I wanted to kill him," Lenny groaned. "I told him he was not only an idiot but he had signed our death warrant. Dilbert, or somebody would be coming for the money."

"What did he say?"

"He said he hadn't thought of that. He tried to call Dilbert at the club but the club was closed. It was too late."

"It was for Dilbert. He was probably dead by then," I said, shivering as I thought of Tom's car plunging into the frigid water.

"Even when I heard about Dilbert's death from Dave," Lenny told me, "I thought it was an accident. I had no idea that everything was coming down so quickly."

"I don't understand why Bob didn't tell you he asked me to go to Duluth for him."

"He knew I'd never let you, but I'm not surprised he asked. He thought you were some sort of a superwoman. He was convinced you could do anything."

"Not everything," I said sadly, knowing that I couldn't bring Bob back or Tom back. I couldn't relieve Lenny of his guilt. And I still hadn't confronted the killers.

"When did you hear from the money's owners?" I asked him.

"Only a few minutes after Bob died. Someone came up behind me at the club and grabbed my neck. At first I thought it was someone trying to, you know, comfort me. Then I realized that if I moved my neck a fraction of an inch, it would be broken."

"What did they say?"

"Consider this a warning. If you don't get the money back to us, the next dead body will be yours."

We were silent for a few minutes, each of us overwhelmed by the situation. There were dead bodies, evil men, and no way out.

Finally I looked at him and asked, "Did Bob set me up?"

"It wasn't a setup," Lenny said. "I think he thought you'd never find out what was in the bag. I think he planned on giving the money back."

"Do you think Grant knew what was really in the bag?"

"I don't know. What do you think?"

"I'm praying he didn't," I told Lenny, not bothering to tell him that lately most of my prayers had gone unanswered.

"As you can tell, I'm in therapy. My therapist, Violet, he tells me that...." Mannie Grand, on-stage at the Comedy Shop & Bait Store, Little Falls, Minnesota.

28

I pulled into a McDonald's drive-thru for a little comfort food — two Big Macs, large fries, a chocolate shake and apple pie. It had only been a few minutes since I had left the condo and Lenny. I was on my way to the police station to meet with Brott.

I hoped to eat enough cholesterol to clog my arteries and stop any blood flow to my brain. I didn't want to be reminded that Grant had vanished, Lenny had helped to vandalize our apartment, Charley was rotting in jail, Bob was still dead, and someone was after me, too.

All I wanted to do at the moment was stuff my face. I didn't want to think anymore. Look where thinking had gotten me so far.

Lenny insisted he had put his life on the line by convincing the killers that I had no idea where the money was. Now that he knew I had the money, I wondered if greed would, once again, rule his heart.

I asked him to tell me who was with him when he broke in. I begged for their names. But no amount of screaming or threats on my part did any good, Lenny steadfastly refused to ID the murderous cretins.

"I've already caused one friend's death. I'm not going to cause another," he argued.

I, of course, refused to tell Lenny where the loot was hidden. As far as I was concerned, the money was my last bargaining tool.

The McDonald's intercom was barely working. I had to repeat my order three times before the guy finally understood. I even had to turn down my Partridge Family Reunion tape so he could hear me.

I bought the tape for ten cents at a garage sale last summer in Fridley. It was a blessing. There's nothing more calming than chewing on fat while listening to David Cassidy sing "Come on, get happy."

As I waited impatiently, I looked in the rear-view mirror and noticed a black limousine parked behind me in line. If this were L.A., I'd be craning my neck to see what movie star was inside. But this was Minnesota and it was most likely a limousine from Mystic Lake Casino.

Thinking about the casino reminded me of my father. It was 2:30 p.m. and his plane should be flying over the Grand Canyon. He was probably playing poker with the person in the next seat. He had agreed to call me no later than 7 p.m. He was sure he'd have the answers I needed by then.

I grabbed the bag of food from the clerk.

"Thanks," I said.

"No problem, Mannie," the drive-thru clerk responded with a grin. I groaned. Sometimes being a local, pseudo-celebrity is embarrassing, especially when you're dealing with your addictions, in this case, food.

I pulled out onto Nicollet Avenue, opened the bag and tossed a hot, greasy French fry into my mouth. Traffic was stop and go. I put my head out the window to see if there was an accident. Instead, I saw an orange triangular road construction sign. I decided to turn right at the next corner.

I'd rather drive down crowded side streets than sit in traffic. I noticed the limo driver felt the same way. Unfortunately, so had dozens of other anxious drivers. I made a quick decision to turn into the nearest alley.

Unlike Chicago or New York, Minneapolis' alleys are sometimes dead-ends, But I know the area because I am into dumpster diving — looking for perfectly good stuff that people throw out. I was driving down the very alley that LaVonne and I found our kitchen table and chairs in. A little scrubbing and a lot of duct tape and the set was as good as used.

I was reaching for more fries when I saw the limo was right behind me. I realized it was not a casino limo and the riders inside were not looking for easy money. I had a feeling these folks earned their money the old-fashioned way. They killed for it.

Just as I thought. Hugs was back in town.

I accelerated and the limo followed suit. It was riding my bumper. I was pushing fifty miles an hour down the narrow, trash-filled alley when the limo smashed into my rear bumper. I was jerked forward and kept driving.

At the end of the alley I plowed right through a cross street without looking. I heard brakes screech all around me. It was a miracle that I made it through alive. I smiled, thinking I was home free. I stopped smiling when I looked in the mirror and saw that the limo had also made it safely across the intersection.

I had to make a decision before the next intersection. The odds of getting across safely were running against me this time.

I looked at the busy street ahead. I apologized to my car and released my seat belt, opened the door, whipped the steering wheel hard to the right and slammed on my brakes. My car turned horizontal blocking the alley. The limo crashed into the side of my car. I saw the driver's head hit the steering wheel. By then I was on the ground running toward Nicollet Avenue and all the traffic. I didn't even bother to take the fries.

I glanced once over my shoulder to see if anyone was following me. No one was. I continued running down Nicollet, my adrenaline pumping hard enough to compensate for my 40 pounds of home-grown insulation. And, being as neurotic as I am, noting that I was burning a few extra calories at the same time.

When I reached the Nicollet Avenue Police Station, two squad cars were already speeding south to the mess I had just created.

I walked up the station's steps, totally prepared to surrender. I knew I faced a long list of potential criminal charges. Leaving the scene of an accident was just the newest.

My ancestors would have been so proud.

At the top of the stairs, I took a deep breath. I told myself it was the last breath of freedom I'd have for a while. I took one more step and then ran like hell, back down the steps.

My Great Uncle Bert escaped three times from the North

Dakota State Prison. As I streaked down Nicollet and into a waiting cab, I understood why my mom always said I reminded her of him.

There was no way I would ever go to jail. Even if I had to continue a life of crime to keep from it.

In the back of the cab I closed my eyes and leaned back into the seat. I refused to open my eyes, because if I did, I knew I would see the ghosts of my ancestors crammed into the cab with me, beaming with pride.

"My therapist tells me I have a lot of anger issues. That really ticks me off!" Mannie Grand, on-stage at Oktoberfest, New Ulm, Minnesota.

2 9

The taxi dropped me at the Radisson. I expected to find LaVonne pampering herself in the suite's Jacuzzi bath. Or maybe gulping bottled waters from the mini-bar, which I'd later have to remember to refill with tap water. I was flush with illegal dough, but I was still a cheapskate.

I walked quickly into the plush lobby and waved to the desk clerk. He, too, was another comedy dropout. They were all over this city — like flies on an outhouse.

The elevator delivered me to the 14th floor which even I knew, was the thirteenth. I slid the plastic key card into the door and walked in unannounced. On the large walnut coffee table was an unopened fruit basket from the hotel.

Earlier that morning, when I reserved the room, I was asked why I needed a room in town. I said that I was working on a movie deal and needed a suite for final negotiations. I was so convincing that I barely noticed how easy it had become for me to lie.

I walked into the suite's master bedroom and saw that LaVonne's bags were not there. It was only a few minutes past check-in time. I told myself that she would arrive shortly. Meanwhile, I needed to get some sleep.

Squeezed under a mainframe all night with Murray meant fending off his suggestions that we have a sexual encounter, even though we couldn't move. And confronting Lenny at the condo and then running for my life from the limo from hell left me exhausted.

Lying down, I automatically clicked the remote to Comedy Central. Most of the stand-up shows were reruns from the eighties. The all too familiar routines dealt with Velcro wallets and jelly shoes. I fell asleep as a still wet-behind-the-ears comic named Drew Carey talked about a liquor store that featured "a drive-thru window for the alcoholic on-the-go."

I had one of those dreams where I didn't know if I was awake or asleep. I kept trying to wake myself up and found that I couldn't.

I was in Las Vegas, running down the strip. It was at night and I was blinded by the neon lights. The heat was sweltering, yet the sidewalks were covered in snow. I kept slipping on patches of ice. Crystal daggers were tumbling off casino rooftops. I was being chased by a troop of demonic, red-plumed, showgirls and a giant clown on stilts who kept pulling my head out of a hat.

I raced by the Monte Carlo Casino. A photo of the world-famous magician, Lance Burton covered the front of the casino. My mother had told me that Burton was a distant relative. I looked up. He was laughing loudly while sawing a showgirl in half. The showgirl was me.

Out of the corner of my eye, I noticed my father tumbling down the white marble staircase to the street. The street was solid ice and he slid by me as if he was on a toboggan. He chuckled when he passed, clutching casino chips and dollar bills in his hands.

I finally woke up. The clock read 6:55 p.m. My head was pounding. I opened my purse and grabbed a bottle of Tylenol. I popped two of the capsules in my mouth and walked to the bathroom and downed an entire glass of water. I was halfway through the glass when I realized that LaVonne had not shown up.

I immediately called the condo to see if LaVonne or Grant were there. They weren't. I called the club, our apartment, and several other places.

I went back to the bathroom sink to take another Tylenol. I looked at my image in the mirror and mouthed the words, "You idiot," and started to cry.

I sat down on the cold tiled floor. Gut-wrenching sobs escaped from the deepest part of my soul. I cried for Bob, Lenny, Charley, Grant, and LaVonne. I also managed to let out a few sobs for myself. For the first time since Bob's death, I allowed the horror of it all to overtake every cell in my body.

In a three-hundred dollar a night suite, paid for by money taken from Bob's stash, I wallowed in self-pity. I marveled at my arrogance. There was nothing but disaster all around me, and I was at the forefront, refusing to change my ways, and leading my friends and family to ruin, even death.

I had a good 15 minute pity session before I stopped crying and started thinking clearly. I stood up, straightened my hair in the mirror, and decided to do what needed to be done.

There was the slight chance that LaVonne was safe and waiting at the club to perform. Maybe even Grant was there. The clock read 7:15. The show would start in 45 minutes.

I took a few minutes to check my voice mail. I had zero messages. My dad hadn't called like he promised to. I immediately called Vegas.

"The Fremont," the operator announced.

"Max Grand," I said.

"Is he a guest?"

"Yes," I answered, looking at the clock's minute hand ticking away.

"I'm sorry but there's no one registered by that name."

"There has to be. My dad promised me that..."

"I'm sorry, but there's no one registered by that name."

"Page him," I told her.

I waited 15 minutes until she came back on the line. No one had answered the page.

I envisioned Dad running wild in Las Vegas. Why had I been foolish enough to tell him where I had hidden the money? Why had I trusted any gambler? Didn't I, of all people. know a gambler is never to be trusted?

I left the plush, useless hotel room and headed down to the Avis-Rent-A-Car counter.

Five minutes later I was in a royal blue Dodge Neon.

The seven minute drive to The Walker Art Center felt like an eternity. I vowed not to stop for anything and I didn't — even when I saw Charley.

Charley was standing at the front window of his little world, smoking a cigarette, and watching nonchalantly as the world and I passed by. He was out of jail. I wondered if his estranged and even stranger relatives put up the bail money. Or maybe Brott had come to his senses and realized that Charley was only guilty of crappy cuisine.

Either way, I didn't have time to find out.

Everything was happening so fast. First, Dilbert was killed in an auto accident in Duluth. Then Bob was murdered on-stage. Charley was arrested. My apartment was destroyed by my friend Lenny and his associates. I was nearly squashed by a speeding limo in a narrow alley. LaVonne, Grant and my dad can't be found at the moment, and Charley, it appeared, was back to making submarines that could sink to the bottom of the ocean.

And, like most comedians do in the worst of times, I kept thinking, "Wow, if I live, I'm going to have a year's worth of material out of this!" I was not only the center of my universe, but everyone else's it seemed.

I parked in front of the building that housed The Guthrie and The Walker Art Center. A gala had brought out high society. They were dressed in elegant evening wear and exiting from long lines of limos that were parked in front of the building. A quick look showed that none of the limos had a smashed front end.

I watched the hoity-toity of Minneapolis ascend the salted steps and then I turned and walked directly into the eleven acre field across the street.

Of course, it's not called a field; it's a sculpture garden. Forty giant sculptures were resting in the garden, covered, for the season, like so many Minnesotans, in snow and ice.

My favorite piece was the giant silver spoon with a red cherry resting in its bowl. It sat in the middle of a 125-foot-amoebae- shaped pond. The sculpture was people friendly enough that, in the spring, children floated sailboats in its water.

I loved looking at the spoon, especially from the bridge I was heading to. The bridge was a walkway that arched over a very busy street, connecting the sculpture garden to Loring Park. When I reached the middle of the bridge, I looked at the small locked metal box with it's computerized keypad, that was attached to the railing. The box contained the controls that lowered the giant holiday ornaments that still dangled over the bridge. From six feet away I could tell by the ice that covered the box that no one had tampered with the ornaments for days.

The money was safe. I didn't need to check it any further.

"Good old dad," I said to myself as I trudged back to the car through the drifting snow. I looked one more time at the string of giant holiday ornaments and then drove off to find LaVonne.

A few stragglers were standing outside the comedy club when I arrived ten minutes later. I parked in the handicapped spot in front of the club. Once I had started breaking the law, I couldn't seem to stop.

The Kid was pacing back and forth in front of the club.

"What's up?" I asked him.

"Dave's throwing a fit. LaVonne and Grant aren't here yet."

"Didn't they call?" I asked, already knowing his answer would be no.

"Dave's gonna have a heart attack when he sees that LaVonne's not with you."

"There's still time. She doesn't go on until 8:15. How much time can you do?"

"Fifteen at the most."

"Do thirty. If she's not here by then, I'll take her spot. By then, Dave can get another headliner down to close the show."

"Don't you want to close it?"

"I can't. I've got a date."

The Kid was right about Dave. When I walked into the club without LaVonne, he grabbed his chest in pain and stared at me.

"Where is she?" Dave mouthed across the room. I shrugged my shoulders and headed back to the dressing room.

The buffet table was bare. Dave hadn't bothered to put out food since the murder. No one would eat it. Behind the empty table was the dressing room's only window. Dark and dusty curtains covered it.

The window was large enough that anyone could have entered or left through it. I pulled back the curtains. The glass was covered in cigarette film. I couldn't see through it. The putty around the window pane, however, caught my eye. It was new. A section of the window had been replaced. The killer had entered and/or exited through the window.

I closed the curtains just as Dave came ranting into the room. "Where in the hell are they?"

"In trouble," I said with such intensity that Dave became silent.

"With who?" he asked, barely able to get the words out.

Instead of answering, I wrapped my arms around myself and gave myself a great big squeeze. Dave looked confused then he understood.

"My God," Dave said, sitting down at the table. "Hugs?"

"Yes," I told Dave. I prayed Dave wasn't acting and was innocent of Hugs' current activities.

"Did you know Milos was still involved with him?" I asked.

"No, I thought Milos quit like I did," he answered. "I thought he was a bad magician and nothing else."

"Not like the old days," I said. I had finally put it together that Milos had hung out at X World because he worked for Hugs. Milos was the second person I had Murray check out. Milos had a stellar rating and numerous platinum credit cards. The only magic around him was black magic.

"Nothing like the old days," Dave answered. "Milos told me he had changed. I believed him because I had to believe that I had changed."

Dave put his head in his hands. We were both silent. I didn't know what to say.

"I've worked hard to keep my reputation spotless," Dave said, looking up at me. "This isn't fair, Mannie."

"Life never is," I said, remembering the many times Dave had said comedy wasn't fair.

"I didn't even know Hugs still came to Minnesota," Dave continued. "I had heard rumors but I haven't spoken to him since the day I was released."

"The same day he rewarded you by selling the club to you for a buck?"

Dave nodded. "I thought that buck turned my life around. It gave me a chance to go legit and leave the crap behind. Are you sure Milos is involved?"

"Positive."

"He had a good cover going," Dave smirked, "The world's crummiest magician."

"But as a bad guy, he's terrific."

"How did Bob know Hugs?" Dave asked. "I never knew anyone more honest than Patterson."

"He was doing a favor for an old friend and ended up holding the wrong bag in the wrong place at the wrong time."

"And the bag was filled with?"

"One million dollars."

"Belonging to Hugs?"

"Either him or Tom Dilbert," I informed Dave.

"Then Tom's death wasn't an accident?" Dave no longer seemed surprised at anything I said.

"He's the old friend of Bob's I was talking about. I have a hotel receipt listing twenty calls Bob made to Dilbert in just one week."

"Was Dilbert dealing drugs?" Dave asked.

I nodded.

"Heroin?" Dave asked.

"Probably, given the amount of money involved. How well do you know the club owner in Duluth?"

"I don't know him. I've only talked to the manager a few times."

"Have you heard any rumors about the club?" I asked.

"Nothing except that the owner overpays the comics."

"He pays the industry standard," I told Dave, and for a change did not bother to add that Dave didn't. "But the club is so small, I always wondered how the place stayed in business. Now I know," I said to Dave.

Dave and I were so engrossed in our little drama that we failed to notice the detective lurking in the doorway, until he spoke.

"Go ahead and finish the scenario, Mannie. You're doing a good job so far."

"Actually, I'd like to hear it from someone else's viewpoint for a change," I told Brott.

He began, "The heroin arrives via the St. Lawrence Seaway.

Duluth is the midway point. It originates in Istanbul on its way to..."

"Seattle," Dave said, already figuring out Dilbert's itinerary.

"Exactly," Brott confirmed. "The freighter is connected to the Chicago crime syndicate."

"The Demopolo Line," I stated.

Brott nodded his head, "I'm impressed that you know as much as you do, Mannie. Why don't you finish?"

"Dilbert was their connection," I told Dave, pointedly ignoring Brott. "He'd carry the heroin back to Seattle."

"Is there anything you haven't figured out?" Brott asked, with what could have been a smile.

"I still have a couple of questions," I replied. "What about Charley?"

"We knew he was innocent all along. Charley agreed to help us. It's The Demopolo empire that is connected."

I breathed a sigh of relief that Charley was free and clear and that Brott was not as big an ass as I thought he was. But my next question was the one I really needed answered. "Where are LaVonne and Grant?"

"I don't know. But one thing I am sure of is that you have to listen to me from now on. No more going off on your own," he said and let it go at that.

I opened my mouth to speak when The Kid came running into the back room and yelled, "It's twenty past eight, what should I do?"

"I've already called Mick and told him to get his butt here as soon as possible," Dave told The Kid. "He can close the show. Mannie, you think you can handle featuring?"

"Yeah, I can do it. But I want off the stage as soon as Mick gets here. I want to find Milos. Maybe he knows where LaVonne and Grant are."

"You're too late," Brott said quietly.

"He's dead?" I moaned.

"He's gone. His apartment is bare."

We could hear the crowd out in front murmuring loudly. They were anxious that the show hadn't started. Dave nodded and The Kid walked on-stage.

While The Kid did his dancing guppy impression, I told Brott everything I knew, except where the money was hidden.

Once again I thought I was clever. And once again, I was dead wrong.

"I'm thinking about going to Sexaholics Anonymous. I hear it's a great place to meet men." Mannie Grand, on-stage, AA Annual Turkey Roast, Hinckley, MN.

30

I've done more than my fair share of bad shows. I've had the microphone turned off as a hint that no one was listening. I've had club owners walk on-stage and whisper in my ear, "Get off!" I've had lit cigarettes tossed at me. But nothing ends a show as quickly as being shot at.

When it was apparent that LaVonne would not show up, The Kid introduced me. I walked to the microphone and the crowd applauded. I opened my mouth to speak but a scream came out instead. A bullet by me and lodged in the wall of The Comedy Box. As the gun exploded one more time, the lights went off, everything went dark. The room was pitch black. And then a small riot began. I could hear tables being turned over, glass breaking, and chairs hitting the floor.

Someone grabbed my arm and pulled me off stage to the rear exit. Thinking it was Brott, I yelled that he was hurting my arm. It wasn't until he opened the door that led into the alley that I realized it wasn't Brott leading me to safety.

It was Milos doing his final trick — making me disappear.

The car Milos pushed me into wasn't the crunched limo he had been driving earlier but my rented Dodge. He had hot-wired the car and moved it to the rear of the club. I was pushed into the backseat, which was already filled by a very large man.

"I've become quite a fan of yours, little lady," he grunted as he tried but failed to move over. Milos drove off into traffic. "Call me Hugs."

"I know who you are," I snapped back. "And when did you see me? I haven't played under a rock yet!"

Hugs laughed. "I like a feisty woman. I'm not talking about your little comedy show. I'm talking about you getting your hands on my money. You're very clever. You've done this before, haven't you?"

"I've never stolen anything. I was money-sitting for a friend," I said as I tried to find room to breathe. Under normal conditions, I'm claustrophobic. Now I was being squashed by three hundred and fifty pounds of sweating, jiggling, murderous blubber.

"You mean a dead friend," Hugs said with a wicked smile. "I don't know if I want to be your pal, Mannie Grand. So many of them end up six feet under."

"Then consider yourself one of my best," I told him.

I wanted to reach up and choke the bastard, but my chubby hands would never reach around his enormous neck. Instead I managed to ask him the one question I hadn't found an answer to.

"How did you do it?"

"It was very simple really. First of all, I consider myself quite a gourmet cook..."

"I can see that," I mumbled, staring at what looked like his ever increasing girth,

"Now, now, now," Hugs muttered, shaking his head. "You mustn't be nasty. You too, Mannie, are a person of size."

Great! I was trapped in a murdermobile with a politically correct homicidal lunatic.

He continued. "I knew about the buffet table in the dressing room. I whipped up my special cyanide and balsamic vinaigrette. One of my men was able to remove a window pane, pull out a sandwich, touch it up and then put it back. No one was the wiser."

"Was it Milos?" I asked, failing to catch Milos' reflection in the rear view mirror.

"Milos doesn't have the stomach for that sort of thing, although I've tried to teach him," Hugs lamented. "But he does have other talents. Did he ever do his card trick for you. The one where...."

"Was your puppet a fat man with a scar across his face?" I interrupted, remembering Charley's story of Santa's shadow.

"Most of my men are, shall I say, larger than life. You'll

190

meet him soon enough," Hugs continued. "He may remind you of someone," he said with a grin.

"I don't understand why, if you were only after Bob, you took the chance of poisoning everyone in the green room?"

"What chance?" Hugs asked, obviously frustrated at my stupidity. "I didn't care who died. I only wanted to send the message that I wasn't to be messed with. Besides, why do you care? Nothing woulda happened to your roommate. Milos said that she was a vegetarian. She was safe all along, unlike now."

"Are she and Grant alive?"

Hugs looked at me wearily and then reached forward and tapped Milos on the shoulder.

"Milos, you're going to like this," he said, giggling at his cleverness. For an evil man, he loved to laugh. "Listen to the joke I'm about to make. I should have been a comedian myself. It's a good one. Are you listening?"

"Sure, Boss," Milos answered. His voice was flat and emotionless. He sounded more like a robot than a human.

"They're tied up right now," Hugs said to me, his body rippling at his remark. Hugs' rolls of fat jostled me with every wave of laughter.

"Very funny," I told him. "You oughta be in show business."

"I am," he said, straight-faced, as if I'd meant what I'd said. "I produce adult movies."

"You mean porn," I said disgusted.

"Of course," he said, like it was a compliment.

"Are they alive?" I asked again.

"At the moment," he answered as he pulled out a cigar, smashing his elbow into my face in the process. He didn't bother to apologize.

"Where is the money, Mannie?" he asked, inhaling deeply on the foulest smelling stogie in the history of the world.

"Let them go and I'll give you the money."

"It's the other way around, Mannie. You give me my money and then I will let LaVonne and Grant go."

"What about me?"

"That I haven't decided yet," he said, flicking an ash on my head.

I tossed my head to knock off the ash and tried to look as mean as possible when I said to him, "I'm the one to bargain with. I'm the one with a million bucks."

I decided instantly to put that line in my act because I've never made two people laugh so loud or as long.

"Do you really think I care about a measly mil?" Hugs asked, wiping tears from his eyes. "The only thing that matters to me is that it belongs to me," he continued. "No one takes anything of mine and gets away with it. No one. You've got two minutes to tell me where the money is, or your friends die."

Hugs pulled out his cell phone and pushed the redial button. "Put her on," he said into the tiny flip top receiver.

He held the phone next to my ear.

"LaVonne?" I whispered.

"Mannie?" she yelled as Hugs yanked the phone away.

He looked at his watch.

"A minute and a half," he said with such evil that even God would have given him the money.

"Do you like art?" I asked him.

He closed the flip phone and put it back in his pocket. "Yes, I do, Mannie, especially Picasso's green period."

"Take us to the Walker," I told Milos.

I leaned back as comfortably as I could in the narrow space between Hugs' obese body and the car door I was crushed against.

Quietly, I prepared to die.

"I've always known that God is on my side, but sometimes I wish He was in front, leading me instead." Mannie Grand, Edina Morningside Congregational Church Women's Club.

31

"Go to L," I told Milos as he stepped out of the car.

"What did you say to me?" Milos responded angrily.

"L, go to the letter L over the bridge," I told him,

I watched him as he trudged down the shoveled garden pathway that, minute by minute, was being covered once again with drifting snow. He reached the walkway at Lyndale and Hennepin Avenue.

Milos stopped on the third step and looked up at the rocking ornaments jigging over the highway. Daily, for over a week, tens of thousands of workers, on their way to downtown, had no idea that a million dollars danced a mere thirty feet above their heads.

The holiday ornaments, designed by international artists, were made of aircraft aluminum. Each one was a letter, spelling out the word HOLIDAZZLE, promoting the spectacular evening parade of lights that happened nightly in Minneapolis during the Christmas season. Each letter was hollow on the inside so that weight could be added, if necessary, to balance against the wind. I was told that the wind had to exceed fifty miles an hour before the additional weight would be needed.

The ornaments were hung by a computerized pulley system of steel cables. The mechanism was designed by the top engineering firm in Minneapolis. There was no way the ornaments were going to come down before they were supposed to. No way. Except when I showed up.

The mechanism to hoist them was a simple coded security system that was known only to the few trusted members of Friends of the Walker who volunteered to help hang the exhibit. LaVonne and I were two of the volunteers.

I was, however, the clumsiest Friend the Walker had ever

193

known. So much so that the museum's artistic installer finally asked me to "just stand at the computerized keypad" and key in the security code that automatically lifted the letters up or down.

The installer, believing that less was more, used such a simple code system that it was impossible to forget. The system needed only three numbers to operate each letter up and down. The letter H was 111, the letter O was 222, and so on. Milos punched 999 to hoist the final L within his reach and pull it toward him. He dropped it on the bridge floor and with a few shots from his gun, the ornament snapped free from the cable. I watched as Milos struggled down the steps with the giant L.

When he reached the car, he placed it on the front seat. The window had to be left open with the top of the letter L reaching out into the street, to get the doors closed.

As we drove off I looked back at the bridge and at the greeting that now spelled HOLIDAZZ E and wondered if in a society where most people's brains had died years ago from television overdose, would anyone notice?

Hugs sat quietly, eating a box of Donut World donuts while Milos drove on I-94 toward St. Paul. He took the first exit past the river to Mississippi Boulevard. The tree-lined street ran along the east side of the river. It was a quiet neighborhood with expensive homes owned by executives from the nearby Ford plant.

He pulled into a circular drive in front of a private mansion. It was the perfect hideaway.

Milos opened my car door and I stepped out.

"Put your hands in front of you," Milos barked, still not looking me in the eye.

I held my hands out and he snapped a pair of handcuffs on them, the same handcuffs he used in his act, except this time there would be no escaping.

We walked to the front door, Hugs puffing with every step. Milos opened the front door and pushed me inside. I stumbled over an oriental rug and landed flat on my face. Hugs laughed at my pratfall.

I peered up from my disadvantaged viewpoint and saw LaVonne's signature Reeboks.

"I always said you should do physical comedy," LaVonne cracked.

"Carol Burnett would have done it better," I told her, tears running down my face as I looked at her.

She and Grant were sitting, tied back to back, on wooden chairs in the middle of a nearly empty room. A long electrical cord wound around LaVonne and Grant like thread on a bobbin. I noticed that the rubber was stripped off in random places and bare wires were showing through. One end of the cord dangled in a bucket of water while the other end was being held by a massive, bearded, scar-faced man who was standing near an electrical outlet.

I looked twice to make sure it wasn't my brother Chet. It wasn't.

I turned to see how Milos was reacting, the same Milos that had wooed and bedded LaVonne. I noticed he wouldn't look at LaVonne.

"Are you okay?" I asked her.

"Just dandy," she said, managing to smile.

I only nodded at Grant. I didn't know what to say to him.

"Hi 'ya, darlin'," Grant said, the Darlin' sounding sincere for a change.

I turned to Hugs. "You have the money. Let them go. They had nothing to do with any of it."

"Guilt by association," Hugs reminded me, holding the ornament and plopping into the only other chair in the room, a large overstuffed recliner. He fell so hard that the recliner jumped backward into the recline position. He couldn't reach the lever to pull himself into a forward position.

The thug who was holding the electrical cord dropped it and rushed to help Hugs. Both he and Milos struggled to pull their boss into an upright position.

"Get me a damn screwdriver!" Hugs yelled and the thug rushed out of the room.

"Here you are, Boss," the gunman said a minute later as he handed him the tool.

As Hugs slowly dismantled the holiday ornament he lost any interest in the rest of us.

195

He placed the screwdriver at the opening on the back of the L. The panel snapped open. It was a simple task, but sweat was dripping down Hugs' bloated, gargoyle face. For a man that big no effort was small.

While he struggled to catch his breath, I asked LaVonne, "Where did he pick you up?"

"Milos was waiting for me outside of the condo. He told me he wanted to talk about Bob."

I looked at Grant. His was half-way across the room but I could tell his face was black and blue. Dried blood was caked on his still gorgeous but bruised forehead.

"You've been here since last night?" I whispered.

"Yep," he answered.

"What do you think the odds are of getting out of here?" LaVonne whispered. I noticed she was trying to wiggle out of the electrical cord.

"Not good," I told her honestly. "Unless Brott shows."

"I still can't believe Milos is involved in this," LaVonne said, glaring at him. "He sent me a dozen roses for Valentine's Day."

"I wonder if he'll send them to your funeral," Grant said as he leaned over and spat on the parquet floor for effect.

The three of us simultaneously turned our heads and stared at Milos. Milos must have felt our hate-filled glares. He turned around slowly to look at us, then turned back. Hugs started pulling $10,000 stacks out of the ornament and tossing them into a leather bag.

"Take a long look at the money!" Hugs demanded as he threw one of the stacks at us. "Was it worth it to steal from me? Have you learned your lesson?"

The hypocrite was making it into a morality play.

"They didn't steal your money," I reminded him. "I did. If you have to kill somebody, kill me."

"I don't have to do anything," he snorted. "I only do what I want to do."

"Then you'll let us go?" LaVonne asked.

"Of course not. I don't have to kill you but I want to kill you. You guys bore me. I don't like being bored. Besides, Mannie, you tell fat jokes. I don't like fat jokes. I find them offensive."

It was pointless to tell him that I only tell them on myself.

Hugs snapped his fingers, a difficult task since they were so fat they could barely reach each other. On cue, the thug walked over and picked up the extension cord plug lying next to the outlet.

"Boss," Milos said, reaching into his pocket, "Let me do Mannie."

"I thought we were friends!" I said to Milos.

"What is it that Dave says?" Milos smirked, "that it's 'show business, not show friendship'?"

Before I could answer, police sirens were blaring and flashing blue lights lit up the room like some cheap chamber of horrors.

Hugs walked over, grabbed me by the arm and dragged me toward the back of the house.

"I'm taking the passageway," he told Milos. "Make sure the job is finished before you leave."

"Will do," Milos said as Hugs yanked me down the hall. I was calling out LaVonne's name as the gunshots rang out.

In the distance I could hear Brott's futile words, "Come out with your hands up."

Several years ago I auditioned for a small role in the movie "Grumpy Old Men" that was being filmed in Minnesota. I envisioned fame and fortune and a nice Screen Actor's Guild check coming my way. My agent assured me that I could get ten thousand dollars for three lines of dialogue.

It was enough for a down payment on a house. I spent that week looking for a house. By the time Ray called and told me the part was not mine, I'd covered several neighborhoods in St. Paul, including the Highland Park neighborhood that runs along the Mississippi River.

My Realtor had overreacted when I told her I was up for a movie role. She had dragged me through one mansion after

197

another while I pleaded to see two-bedroom bungalows that cost seventy thousand dollars max.

One of the estates she insisted on viewing was located on Mississippi Boulevard. She told amusing tales of estates built in the 1920s, furnished with copper tubs built especially for making bathtub gin. She spoke of homes large enough to be either bordellos or convents. There were rumors, she said, that a few of the homes had private tunnels that led to the Mississippi River, where booze drifted down from the north.

By the late thirties, the criminal activities had died away and activists jailed. The private docks were torn down and public parks established instead. And, according to legend, the tunnels were filled in and boarded up a long time ago.

But I found at least one tunnel had survived, the one that Hugs and I were trudging through.

It was pitch black except for the weakening flashlight beam Hugs carried in one hand. In his other hand he held the money-filled satchel.

"Keep walking," he grunted from behind me, each word barely heard over his exaggerated breathing. "Keep moving."

I figured it was a couple of hundred yards to the end of the tunnel. Water dripped down on my head. What once had been a wooden floor had deteriorated into partial mud and I could feel my feet sinking into the mire.

With each step, I felt like I was sinking deeper into my grave. Besides my basic terror, I was having a full-fledged anxiety attack. I was trembling, sweating, my mind racing. My chest felt as if Hugs was sitting on it.

Over and over, I kept hearing the gunshots in my head.

I didn't care about dying anymore. I deserved to die — Grant and LaVonne were dead because of me.

We walked for what seemed like hours, but I knew it was only a few minutes.

Suddenly, I tripped over something cold and hard. We had reached the end of the passageway.

I pulled myself up from the cold, metal monster I had just landed on.

"Get on," Hugs said.

"Where?" I asked.

"There," he said as he lowered the beam on what looked like a giant metal egg with a leather chair inside it.

It was a two-seater motorcycle, like the ones in World War II movies, the kind with a passenger sidecar.

Hugs, who was at least two hundred pounds overweight, was going to drive the ice-covered streets of St. Paul on a motorcycle, and I was going along for the ride.

Hugs pushed me into the sidecar and pulled the seat belt tightly around me, trapping my arms.

He wasn't strapping me in for safety reasons. He had put the money in my lap.

"Lose the bag and you die," he told me.

"Save the money and I still die," I managed to squeak out. Hugs grunted and shone his light on the exit. I tried to wiggle out of the seatbelt but couldn't. I was trapped.

Hugs snorted and groaned as he pulled back the boarded-up tunnel's exit. Suddenly the river was in front of me. Under other circumstances I would have admired the pine covered banks leading down to the Mississippi. Moonlight reflected off the ice.

"Lord," I prayed silently as I heard Hugs gasping for air, "if he's meant to die of a heart attack in this lifetime, let it be now."

But, instead of dying, he waddled, as fast as he could, back to the motorcycle and started the engine.

We flew off into the night, the BMW motorcycle carrying its heavy load with ease. The tunnel entrance was a short ten feet from a riverside park's parking lot. Even in the darkness I recognized the lot. It was only a block from the house we had just left. Hugs had no choice but to drive down the street where the police were.

I watched the BMW's speedometer hit fifty miles an hour as Hugs drove up the incline. When we reached the street, he drove onto it without looking either way. I stopped looking at the speedometer when it hit eighty.

It was twenty seconds before police sirens sounded and flashing lights were closing in from behind. I should have felt a little comfort at that, but I didn't. Instead, I felt like I was on the amusement park ride from hell.

Hugs raced down Mississippi Boulevard, ignoring the oncoming traffic. As far as Hugs was concerned, the center line was his.

I hoped that each passing car would see me, attached to the side of the motorcycle like an unwilling parasite.

The blue lights were getting closer. I was getting more frightened. I was terrified that Hugs would activate a release button and I would go flying off into the squad car behind us.

When we reached the Ford Parkway bridge, Hugs turned left onto the bridge. He accelerated once again and turned to look at the speeding cars behind him.

He obviously hadn't taken drivers ed in high school. Anyone could have told him he should have used his rearview mirror instead. It pays to follow the rules.

In the few seconds it took for him to turn around, a familiar looking dark brown truck came rumbling across the bridge. The driver was driving cautiously in his own lane. Unfortunately, it was the same lane that Hugs was in — and me.

When I saw the truck heading directly toward me, I screamed louder than I thought humanly possible. I didn't want to be delivered into the next world by UPS.

Hugs saw the truck hurtling toward us and swerved the motorcycle into the other lane, losing control on the ice.

The motorcycle roared toward the bridge railing and flew over the edge, straight into the icy waters fifty feet below.

I was waiting to see my life pass in front of my eyes. Instead, Brott passed in front of them.

His squad car had pulled ahead as Hugs hit the metal railing. The sidecar caught on the railing and was ripped from the motorcycle. It took one second for the cycle and Hugs to go over the bridge. I, still trapped, went skidding down the roadway like a run-away tilt-a-whirl.

The impact of the crash had ripped open my seat belt. The money bag flew out of the sidecar and skipped over the edge of the bridge. It opened in mid-air and stacks of money followed Hugs into the river. Some of the stacks landed on ice chunks and floated down the Mississippi as if they were on a winter cruise. The rest sank to the muddy bottom.

My hands, still handcuffed together, clutched the front of my swirling metal egg death-trap. I ended up bumping off the railings enough times to slow down. When I finally stopped rolling, I was soon surrounded by cop cars.

The first one out of a car was Brott. LaVonne and Grant were next. They were running toward me, their arms opened wide.

I couldn't have been more surprised or happier, except when the car's final rider jumped out and joined them running.

"Mannie!" Dad yelled as he ran toward me, casino chips falling out of his pocket.

"Oh, wow," Mannie Grand, Minneapolis - St. Paul International Airport, Gate 15, after Grant Cuddler kisses her good-bye.

3 2

Forty-eight hours after I had bounced along the Ford Parkway Bridge, I was nestled in the safety of our apartment, still shaking. LaVonne refused to step outside our door.

Grant had left that afternoon. I dropped him off at the airport. He was performing in Chicago that night and promised to give me a call after his show. He had also promised me he'd check out Gamblers Anonymous. On the way to Minneapolis/St. Paul International, he finally told me about his nervous breakdown at the Tropicana in Las Vegas. His reckless gambling had caused it.

He said he had given up trying to make it to the top years ago. "Why should I even bother?" he asked. "I'll just leave every penny I earn at the craps table."

But after almost losing his life, he had second thoughts about the universe giving us all second chances. I convinced him that G.A. might just show him how to get that chance.

My dad was at the apartment. I had promised him dinner. He and LaVonne were trying to put our stereo system back together. He swore he could fix it, and if anybody could, he could. He was good at fixing things.

Dave Olson was also there. I've known Dave for eighteen years and this was the first time I had ever invited him over. Sitting on the kitchen were the two bottles of Merlot and dozen roses that he had brought.

You never really know someone, I reminded myself.

"Can I do anything to help?" LaVonne asked as she walked back into the kitchen.

"Nah, everything's under control," I answered as I slid the four filet mignons under the broiler rack. The twice-baked potatoes were keeping warm on the top of the stove. Charley had sent a Greek salad and Baklava for dessert with a note saying his deli was busier than ever. The bad publicity had actually brought in customers.

The dinner was my final fling. There was only $2,434 left in the "expense account" I had lifted from Bob's bag of money. According to the newspaper, the million bucks was lost in the Mississippi. No one except LaVonne and I knew that thousands of dollars had been liberated.

"Your dad seems like a cool guy," Dave said, practicing small talk that wasn't connected to the club.

"He's the best," I smiled.

"I heard he saved your life," Dave told me.

Rumors, even good ones, traveled fast.

"Yeah, he did. But so did Brott," I said, surprised that my eyes filled with tears. Both LaVonne and I had been crying off and on all day long.

"Don't forget about Milos," LaVonne sighed.

"Never," I answered. Milos was the reason LaVonne was sitting across from me.

"Why did Tom Dilbert leave the money in the condo?" Dave asked. We were all still trying to fit the pieces of the puzzle together.

"He was setting Cuddler up for the fall. Dilbert was planning to steal the money from Hugs and blame it on Grant. Dilbert didn't know that Grant had left a message on Dilbert's answering machine that Bob Patterson would deliver the money. He didn't know about Bob because Milos intercepted the message and then told Hugs."

"So when Dilbert tried to pin the missing money on Grant, Hugs knew Dilbert was lying."

"And that's when Hugs killed him and went after Bob."

"Exactly."

"How did your dad help?" Dave asked, lowering his voice so that Dad wouldn't hear. He could tell that my father wasn't the kind of man who liked to boast.

"I told Dad that I wanted him to go to Vegas to get information," I said as I opened a bag of heat and serve rolls.

"Once there, he realized I also sent him out-of-town for his own protection. He decided to do what he could to protect me instead. He immediately flew back to Minneapolis and headed straight to the police. He told them everything. The police watched Milos and I pick up the money at The Walker."

"Why didn't Brott arrest Hugs and Milos right then and there. Your life was in danger," Dave said.

"Brott said that if they arrested Hugs and Milos at the Sculpture Garden, he was afraid we'd never find LaVonne and Grant alive. He wanted Hugs to lead him to his hideaway. Brott assumed correctly that LaVonne and Grant would be there."

"Did Brott know that Milos would end up on your side?" Dave asked.

"None of us knew that," I said sadly. "I don't even know if Milos knew until the last minute."

As soon as Hugs had dragged me kicking and screaming out of the room, Milos took one more look at LaVonne. He blew her a kiss and lifted the gun. He shot the bearded thug that had killed Bob and then turned the gun on himself. Milos still loved LaVonne after all.

I'll never know if Milos would have bothered saving me.

"What about your brother? Is he a gang member?"

"No. Hugs tried to recruit Chet and other homeless people years ago. When Chet turned him down, he had his henchmen slash Chet's face to change his mind. Fortunately, it didn't work. But Hugs was still news on the streets. Chet heard it and knew I was in over my head."

"Have they recovered all the money yet?" Dave asked.

I turned away from Dave. I didn't want him to see the slight smile that I couldn't stop. I reached into the broiler and turned the steaks over. When they were done, we'd be feasting on beef that cost over fourteen dollars a pound.

"They found some of the money," I told him, " Most of it is resting at the bottom of the Mississippi."

"And you guys aren't in trouble with the law," Dave said as he shook his head.

"For what?" LaVonne asked. She's so good at acting innocent.

"Why would I be in trouble?" I asked, crossing my fingers behind my back. "I was holding money for a friend. How did I know it was drug money?"

"Even Lenny's in the clear," LaVonne added. "The fact that a slew of comedians might have been killed has become something of a public relations nightmare for the police department."

"Brott is even acting nice toward us," I told Dave.

"To some of us more than others," LaVonne smiled. She knew that Brott and I were meeting for coffee later. When he had called, I asked him if he wanted more information. He said no, he only wanted to see me. You never really know someone, I thought again.

"The TV's working," Dad announced as he walked into the room.

"That's great!" I told him. "We'll watch it after dinner."

"Mannie, if you want I can come over tomorrow and work on your record player."

"It's called a stereo now, Dad. I appreciate it, but LaVonne and I already have plans for tomorrow."

LaVonne's poker face didn't give us away.

We didn't tell my dad or Dave that we planned on spending the next day shopping. This time we wouldn't buy a thing on clearance. Why should we? We had over two thousand dollars in our pockets.

Forty-eight hours later, LaVonne and I were watching the Channel 11 evening news. I had just finished packing for my Missouri tour and wanted to check the weather forecast. I was heading to St. Louis to meet with the comedy team of Lewis and Clark. For a change, I was glad to get away. We were just ready to click off the news when the anchorman made his final report.

"There's a heartwarming story coming out of Minneapolis today that proves every day can be Christmas. This morning, nearly two thousand dollars worth of toys were left at the doorstep of the TOYS FOR TOTS headquarters. The only thing we know about the donor is that he left a card signed with only his first name. Thanks, Bob, wherever you are."

Acknowledgments

I am forever-in-debt to my writers' group and close friends of 14-plus years, Marjory Myers-Douglas, Mary Rogers, and Zola Thompson. Thank you to my editor and re-discovered friend, Pat Morris, I am sincerely grateful to those who have supported this project - April Anderson, Laura Roberts-Andrejasich, Nancy Beck, Kathleen Brogan, Mark Dennis, Steve Dennis, Jean Fox, Craig Hergert, Mary Hirsch, Maxine Jeffris, Dean Johnson, John Kudrle, Codey Livingood, Marit Livingood, Sharon Rush, Peter Schnieder, Sharron Stockhausen, and Susan Vass. I am always grateful to LaVonne Heintz, wherever she is, for supporting my dreams at the very beginning. I would like to share my awe and appreciation of my cover artist who continues to surprise me with her talent.

A heartfelt thank you to the audiences I have made laugh through out the years.

And a sincere apology to the audiences I didn't.

About The Author

Pat Dennis is an award-winning author and comedian. Her fiction has been published in such magazines as *Woman's World* and *Minnesota Monthly*. Her best-selling collection of culinary mystery short stories, *Hotdish To Die For*, won a Merit Award from Midwest Independent Publishers Association. The collection has been featured on NBC, CBS, ABC, public television, radio, and other local affiliates. Her short story, *Bronte Rides The Bingo Bus*, won First Place in the SASE/ Borders Short Fiction Contest. Her numerous comedy performances include Dudley Rigg's, "What's So Funny About Being Female?" and "Minnesota's Funniest Women" at Knuckleheads at the Mall of America. Pat resides in the Twin Cities area with her loving husband and somewhat loving cats.